Absent Without Leave

》》》》》》》》》》 《《《《《《《《《《《

Heinrich Böll

Absent without
LEAVE

Two Novellas by Heinrich Böll

TRANSLATED FROM THE GERMAN BY

LEILA VENNEWITZ

NORTHWESTERN UNIVERSITY PRESS

EVANSTON, ILLINOIS

》》》》》》》》》》 《《《《《《《《《《《

Northwestern University Press
Evanston, Illinois 60208-4210

Printed in the United States of America

ISBN 0-8101-1231-0 cloth
ISBN 0-8101-1209-4 paper

TRANSLATOR'S ACKNOWLEDGMENT

I am deeply indebted to my husband,
William Vennewitz, for his assistance in this translation.

LEILA VENNEWITZ
Vancouver, Canada

»»» C O N T E N T S «««

1

ABSENT WITHOUT LEAVE
a novella

91

ENTER AND EXIT
a novella in two parts:
When the War Broke Out
When the War Was Over

Absent without Leave

a novella

I

Before coming to the actual subject of this work (work
to be understood here in the sense of clockwork), to the
Bechtold family, of which I became a member on September 22, 1938, shortly before five in the afternoon, at
the age of twenty-one, I would like to submit a few facts
about myself which I trust will be misunderstood and
arouse suspicion. The time is ripe to air at least some of
the secrets to which I owe an upright demeanor, a sound
mind in a sound body (although the latter is debat-
able), discipline and constancy, qualities which my
friends deplore and my enemies resent, and which may
represent a source of strength to unbiased, impartial
citizens in an age which demands of each one of us
perseverance at, in, or on behalf of: Here the reader
may fill in, as if he were completing a printed form,
whatever seems most essential at the moment: readiness

to defend, to attack, to aid, to act with, on behalf of, in FC, JC, MSC, NATO, SEATO, the Warsaw Pact, East *and* West, East *or* West; the reader is even entitled to harbor the heretical notion that the compass also indicates such cardinal points as North and South; however, he is also at liberty to insert what are known as abstract terms: faith, lack of faith, hope, despair, and to those who feel they are totally deprived of any guiding hand and lacking both concrete and abstract terms, I recommend the most extensive encyclopedia available from which he can pick out anything he fancies from Aardvark to Zwingli. . . .

The reason I have not mentioned either the lenient church of believers or the intolerant church of unbelievers is not caution but sheer terror that I might be recalled to duty: the word duty ("I am on duty," "I have to go on duty," "official duty") has always alarmed me.

As long as I can remember, but particularly since that September 22, 1938, on which I underwent a kind of rebirth, my aim in life has been to become unfit for duty. I have never quite achieved this goal, although I have been close to it. I was prepared at any time not only to swallow pills, suffer injections, pretend I was crazy (most miserable failure of all), I even had people whom I did not regard as my enemies but who had reason to regard me as their enemy, shoot me in the right foot, push a sliver of wood through my left hand (not directly, but through the agency of a stoutly built German railway car that was blown up with me in it), I even had myself shot in the head and hip; dysentery, malaria, common diarrhea, nystagmus and neuralgia, migraine (Meunière) and mycosis—nothing worked. Each time the doctors made me fit for duty again. Only one doctor made any serious attempt to certify me as unfit for duty; the only good thing that led to was a ten-day tour of *official duty,* with official travel documents, official ration book, official hotel billeting in Paris— Rouen—Orléans—Amiens—Abbeville. A nice eye specialist (nystagmus) wangled the trip for me; armed with a detailed list I was to buy for him *les oeuvres complètes de Frédéric Chopin* who, he confessed, was to him what absinthe was to the early symbolists. He was not angry, just sad and disappointed, when the one series I was unable to complete was the waltzes, and the absence of Valse No. 9 in A-sharp, which I had not been able to find anywhere, was a bitter blow. I got nowhere by quickly concocting a sociology of sorts and explaining at great length that of course this piece was prized by the piano-playing ladies of every city, town and village for its exquisite melancholy; he was still disappointed, and when I suggested he send me to unoccupied France, when I explained—again at great length —that undoubtedly Marseilles, Toulouse, Toulon would not be influenced by the sultry inland air that made the Valse No. 9 in A-sharp such a sought-after drug—he gave a knowing smile and said: "I bet that's just what you'd like." I expect he meant that down there it would be easy for me to desert, and if he wanted to prevent that happening it was certainly not because he begrudged me the opportunity (we had played chess together for nights on end, we had discussed desertion for nights on end, he had played Chopin to me for nights on end), but probably because he did not want me to make a fool of myself. I solemnly swear that I would not have deserted down there in the South, for the simple reason that I had a loving wife waiting for me at home, later on wife and child, later still only a child. In any case, his efforts to cultivate my nystagmus abated, and a few days later he handed me over as "an interesting case"—I resented his using this term, it was the lowest form of betrayal—to the consulting ophthalmologist of the Western Division of the Army, whose shoulder braid I found as depressing as his aura of professional importance. Prompted by revenge, I suppose (he must have sensed my dislike), he injected my eyes for two days in a row with some infernal stuff that made it impossible for me to go to the movies. I could not see more than ten or twelve feet, and I have always preferred sitting far back at the movies. Anything further than ten or twelve feet away appeared distorted and fuzzy, and I wandered around Paris like a Hänsel without Gretel's comforting hand. I was not rendered

unfit for duty, I was merely sent back to my unit as
"exempt from shooting." My superior (delightful
word, it melts in my mouth) simply altered two letters
in the spelling and sentenced me to a job at which I had
already had a good deal of experience. Among veterans
this occupation is commonly known as "shit duty." I
hesitate to use this term and do so only for the sake of
historical accuracy and out of respect for all technical
jargon.

I had obtained my first experience in this honorable
fecal calling three years previously, during spade drill,
when, at the command "Down spades," I had suddenly
—because up to then I had been quite skillful—struck
my superior officer in the back of the knee with the edge
of the spade. When I was asked what my profession
was, I answered truthfully and with naïve insouciance
that I was an "arts student," and on the basis of the
universally acknowledged German respect for every
common and uncommon variety of intellectual activity,
I was condemned to work in the ordure field, "to make a
man of me."

So I still remembered how to put together a ladle out
of an old lard pail, a pole, some wire and nails, I was
also familiar with the physics and chemistry involved,
and for several weeks, between seven a.m. and half-past
twelve, and between 2:30 and 5:30 in the afternoon, I
walked through a straggling French village not far

from Mers-les-Bains, a lard pail in each hand, and fertilized the neat vegetable patch of the battalion commander. This man, in civilian life the principal of a rural elementary school, had planted an exact replica of his school garden at home: cabbages, onions, leeks, carrots, a sizable colony of corn stalks ("for my chicks"). What embarrassed me about this battalion commander was his habit when off duty of turning into "a regular guy," of coming over to "strike up a conversation" with me. In order to prevent this *faux pas* —superiors who turn into regular guys have always revolted me—in order to preserve my dignity and draw his attention to his own, it was necessary every time for me to sacrifice a whole bucketful of ordure, tipping it over at his feet, taking care not to give the impression of clumsiness and yet at the same time not making my real purpose *too* obvious, for my aim was to make him understand our difference in rank. I had nothing against him personally; he was an object of complete indifference to me. It is clear that, in the execution of even the humblest calling, style is vitally important. In any event, by spreading a belt of ordure around I managed to stay out of his reach. The fact that he was so overcome by nausea (a few minute particles splashed into his face) that he suffered a bilious attack, is not my fault: as a captain in the reserve he shouldn't have been *that* sensitive. His mistress (whom he undoubtedly would not have been able to afford at home, she was listed in the battalion payroll as a mess aid on special *duty*) consoled him by playing the piano as he lay in bed—the Valse No. 9 in A-sharp, as it happened, and I suspected her, and still suspect her, of being the one who snatched the music from under my very nose in Abbeville, thus ruining my nystagmus career. On mild autumn evenings she sometimes went for walks through the village, dressed all in mauve and carrying a riding whip; pale, more corrupted than corrupt, the personification of Madame Bovary collaborateuse.

At this point the patient reader may pause for breath. I shall not digress, I shall regress, I solemnly promise: the subject of ordure has not yet been quite exhausted, while we have finished with Chopin—qualitatively at least, although quantitatively I shall have to resort to him now and again, if only for the sake of literary composition. It won't occur again. Humbly I beat my breast, the quantitative measure of which can be ascertained from my tailor but the quality of which is so hard to define. I would like nothing better than to introduce myself here with a clear statement relevant to my duty; for instance—political affiliation: democrat, but would this still apply to someone who has refused to be "a regular guy" with army captains, someone who, be it only with ordure, keeps his distance? Or take another category: religious affiliation. It would be easy to use one of the common abbreviations; the choice is limited: Prot., Luth., Calv., Cath., R.C., Orth., Isr., Hebr., "other." I have always found it embarrassing that religions, which their adherents and others have been struggling to define for 2,000, for 6,000—for 400 years, should be reducible to pitiful abbreviations, but even if I wanted to I could not supply a single one of these abbreviations.

I must not proceed without revealing an error which amounts almost to a congenital defect and has involved me in all kinds of difficulties and misunderstandings. My parents, united in a mixed marriage, were far too devoted for one to burden the other with the ordeal of deciding once and for all which church I should belong to (it was only at my mother's funeral that I found out that she had been the Protestant one). They had worked out a highly involved system of mutual respect: on Sundays they would take turns for one to go to Trinity Church and the other to St. Mary's; a kind of exalted religious courtesy, whose nicest little touch was that every third Sunday neither of them went to either church. Although my father assured me repeatedly that I had been baptized into the Christian community, I never took part in any religious instruction. Though I am getting on for fifty, I am still groping in the dark; the Income Tax Department, inasmuch as I do not pay church taxes, has me listed as an atheist. I would like very much to become a Jew so as to get rid of that embarrassing "other" in this column, but my father feels that then when he dies and finally exposes the secret, I would have to resign from the Jewish community, and that would be open to misinterpretation. So I prefer to call myself unofficially a "coming Christian," which exposes me to the unfounded suspicion of being an Adventist. As far as religion is concerned I am an unknown quantity, a cause for despair, a thorn in the flesh for the atheists, an "obscure case" for the Christians, not eager to proclaim a faith, immature, too courteous toward my deceased mother; after all—as one man of God recently put it—"Courtesy is not a theological category." Which is a pity, otherwise I might easily be a very religious man.

I wish to present this work, not only as far as I am concerned but also in regard to all other persons appearing in it, less as a completed record than as one of those coloring books with which we are all familiar from our happy childhood days: you could get them for a nickel (at the dime store they were even two for a nickel). They were the standard gift of unimaginative and parsimonious aunts and uncles who simply took it for granted that you owned a paintbox or a set of crayons. In these books only some of the lines were drawn in, and often only dots which you joined together to form

lines. Freedom of expression was yours even in the joining of the lines, and *full* freedom of expression could be
enjoyed by filling in the spaces with color. A figure
whose collar or tonsure obviously suggested a priest
could, while permitting of many variations, be colored
with the standard clerical black, but you could also
make him white, red, brown or even purple. Since the
top half of each page left room for further artistry,
you could draw in the head covering, making it anything from a biretta to a miter. You could also turn him
into a rabbi or, by the addition of white clerical bands,
clearly indicate a post-Reformation denomination. If
all else failed you got hold of an encyclopedia, opened it
at "priest's clothing," and knew then exactly which
neck, head and foot covering (such as sandals for a
Franciscan monk) were required in order to achieve the
man of God you had in mind. It was also possible, of
course, simply to ignore the suggested "priest" in his
meager outlines and construct a bumpkin, baker or bar-
tender, or a Caesar, chiromancer or clown. A figure
armed with a ticket punch, its dots and outlines somewhat obviously indicating a ticket-taker, could be
turned into a streetcar, train or bus conductor, and if
with a few deft strokes (not prohibited by the printed
instructions) you turned the ticket punch into a pipe,
or extended it into the crook of a walking stick, you
could make him into a museum guard, a factory jani-

tor, or a veteran gallantly marching along at a regimental reunion. I for one made full use of this metamorphic scope and horrified my mother by transforming figures that were clearly supposed to be chefs into surgeons at operations, by turning the spoon into a scalpel and making the cap look flatter by widening the face. With female outlines I was even more ruthless: because I was so good at drawing grilles, I turned all these figures into nuns, though I must admit my father sometimes mistook them for ladies in a harem.

There is no question about it: a few outlines, given a certain direction by a few skillfully scattered dots, permit of much greater freedom than the yearned for absolute freedom, for this absolute freedom is at the mercy of the imagination of the individual who, as we all know, has no ideas at all, none whatever, and in whom a blank sheet of paper can provoke just as much despair as that empty hour when the television set is out of order. It is not merely to blur my portrait that I have devoted a few parting tears and thoughts to the dying art of coloring. Now that our children have learned to take blank paper and paint exhibition-level pictures, and at the age of fourteen can discuss Kafka, some adult exhibitions have become as embarrassing as some adult literary comments. Obviously a lamb that is truly naïve, as well as capable of interpreting the oracle's smile, knows how to arrange its entrails, before it is slaughtered, in an interesting and ambiguous pattern, and by previously swallowing pins, needles and paper clips, party and other badges or church tax statements, how to furbish the contents of its woolly fleece; while a lamb that is neither naïve nor capable of interpreting the oracle's smile offers its entrails "just as they are": pathetic little intestines, from which it is impossible to conjure up any kind of future at all. I therefore offer a few strokes, a few dots, which the reader is at liberty to use as an outline to decorate the brickwork of the memorial chapel which this little work is intended to become: he may apply it to the bare walls in the form of either a fresco or a graffito, or even a mosaic.

Foreground and background will be left quite free: for raised fingers, hands wrung in indignation or despair, for shaken heads, lips compressed in grandfatherly severity and superior wisdom, for furrowed brows, held noses, burst collars (with or without ties, clerical bands, etc.), for St. Vitus' dance and foaming mouths, discarded or scattered gall or kidney stones for whose emergence into the light of day I may be to blame.

Like a miserly uncle or a thrifty aunt, I take for granted the possession of a paintbox or a set of crayons. Those who have nothing but a pencil, a ballpoint, or the remains of some ink, are free to try it in monochrome.

In place of the dual, triple or quadruple levels of ambiguity which may be missed by some, I suggest multiple levels: the humus of the ages, which we can have for nothing, the rubble of history, to be had for even less than nothing. I have no objection to anyone extending my, that is, my model's feet, or adding an archeologist's hook to my hand, so as to dredge up all kinds of amusing objects: one of Agrippina's bracelets, the one she lost during a brawl with some drunken Roman sailors of the Rhine fleet—she was drunk too— at the precise spot where my parents' house used to stand (and now stands again), or one of St. Ursula's shoes, perhaps even a button from General de Gaulle's coat, ripped off by the enthusiastic mob and washed down into modern sewers, thence into historically more interesting layers. What *I* have fished out so far has been well worth the trouble: a sword pommel belonging to Germanicus Caesar when he pulled too violently, almost wildly (perhaps even hysterically) at his scabbard in order to display to a muttering crowd of Roman-Germanic mutineers the sword with which he had so often led them to victory. A well-preserved lock of Germanic hair, which I was able without the slightest difficulty to identify as originating from the head of Thumelicus, together with a number of other objects which I will not enumerate so as not to arouse the envy of tourists and their desire to dredge and rake.

But now we will neither digress nor regress: we will forge straight ahead and at last draw near a certain reality—Cologne. A stupendous heritage, an immense historical cargo (immense in proportion to its latitude, anyway). Let us, as sailors say, "clear the decks" before we sink down into the mire of history. Mere mention of the fact that from here, in order to win a fame that was both illusory and delusory, Caligula deliberately provoked hostile engagements with the Tencterians and Sugambrians would be enough to swamp us and make us try in vain to erect dikes. To penetrate to the Caligula layer, the fourth from the bottom, I would have to remove all the upper layers entirely, some twelve or so, and the top one would already be a mass of rubble, stucco, broken furniture, human bones, steel helmets, gas-mask containers, buckles, squashed or trodden flat only on the surface, and how would I explain to the younger generation—apart from everything else—what the inscription on the buckle, "*Gott mit uns*," can have meant?

Since I have already admitted to being born in Cologne (a fact which will make Leftist, Rightist, Center and Diaspora Catholics wring their hands in despair, as it will Rhineland and other Protestants, as well as doctrinarians of every hue, in other words: practically everyone), I would like, so as at least to encourage suspicion as well as misunderstanding, to offer a

selection of at least four streets as the one in which I
was born: Rheinau-Strasse, Grosse-Witsch-Gasse, Filz-
engraben, and Rhein-Gasse, and in case anyone should
feel I have moved my parents' house perilously close to
those environs where Nietzsche foundered but Scheler
flourished, let me inform him that in none of these
streets was or is that calling pursued of which the
drunken Roman sailors took Agrippina to be an ex-
ponent, and should practiced snoopers set out to try
and determine where Agrippina *really* got into a brawl,
where Thumelicus *really* landed, where Germanicus
gave his famous speech, then I will merely add, in order
to compound the confusion, that when visitors come
across the ivory box in my glass cabinet and ask me
whose hair is inside it, I sometimes ascribe its origin to
the head of one of Lochner's models or St. Engelbert:
in holy places like Cologne, such mistakes are permissible and customary.

When asked about my racial background I frankly
supply the following information: Jewish, Germanic,
Christian. The central link in this trinity may be replaced by any one of the numerous pure or mixed racial
categories that Cologne has to offer: but whether it be
pure Samoyed, mixed Swedish-Samoyed, or Slovenian-
Italian, I cannot sacrifice the two outer brackets—
Jewish-Christian—holding my racial blend together;
those who are none of these things, or only one of them

(mixed Slavic-Germanic only, for instance), are hereby declared fit for active duty and ordered to report for military inspection forthwith. The requirements are well known: properly washed, and ready at any time to strip to the skin.

II

This concludes the interior outline; let us pass on quickly to the exterior: height—five foot eleven; coloring—medium fair; weight—normal. Distinguishing features: slightly lopsided walk due to hip wound.

When on September 22, 1938, about four forty-five in the afternoon, I boarded a Number 7 streetcar in front of the main railway station in Cologne, I was wearing a white shirt, olive-drab trousers recognizable to the informed (of those days) as part of a uniform. Anyone who did not come too close, in other words could not detect my odor, would have said I looked "quite all right." A source of surprise to those who knew me (because all my friends are aware that, from my paternal great-great-grandfather, who came from a village near Nimwegen, I suffer from anancastia (obsessional handwashing), yet another detail leading to a limbo of uncertainty and infinity)—and probably for that reason rather touching—were my dirty fingernails. For the dirty nails I offer a simple explanation: as a sharer in our national destiny and a member of that compulsory mutual fellowship whose uniform I was supposed to be wearing (as soon as the train pulled out I had taken it off in the washroom and packed it away in my suitcase, except for the trousers which, for reasons of decency, and the shoes, for reasons of necessity, I could not remove)—in this compulsory mutual fellowship I had adopted the common practice, when our nails were inspected for cleanliness before dinner, of cleaning them quickly with a fork. So that day, which I spent almost entirely in the train (no money to eat in the dining car, so no fork to clean my nails with) I was still at large, late in the afternoon, with dirty nails. To this day, twenty-seven years later, at both formal and informal meals, I have to restrain myself from quickly cleaning my nails with a fork, and I have often provoked angry looks from waiters who took me for a boor, but sometimes respectful looks from people who took me for a snob. In acquainting the reader with this habit, I would like to point out the ineradicable effects of military training. So when your children come to table with dirty nails, the best thing to do is to pack them off right away to the army. Should the reader be overcome with nausea, or be concerned about hygiene, let me add that of course I and my fellow-sharers in our national destiny wiped our forks on our trouserlegs and then rinsed them off in the hot soup. Now and again when—as rarely happens—I am alone, that is, neither accompanied nor watched over by my mother-in-law or my grandfather, nor having a bite to eat with business friends on the terrace of the Café Reichard, I reach naturally and instinctively for the fork and do indeed use it to clean my nails. I was recently asked by an Italian tourist sitting at the next table whether this was a German custom, a fact which I unhesitatingly confirmed. I even referred him to Tacitus and the well-known expression in Italian Renaissance literature, *"forcalismo teutonico"*—he made a note of it then and there in his travel diary, and when he whispered again: *"formalismo tautonico"?* I let it pass, because I thought it sounded so nice.

So except for my dirty nails I really looked quite all right. Even my shoes had been shined. Not by my own hand (I have consistently refused to do this) but by the hand of one of my fellow-sharers in our national destiny, who knew no other way of expressing his gratitude for services I had rendered to him. Money, tobacco, material objects of any kind—these he was tactful enough not to offer me; he was illiterate, and I wrote ardent letters for him to two girls in Cologne, whose address, although not far from my parents' house (only two to seven streets away) was in a milieu totally unfamiliar to me (in fact, the very one that had caused the mix-up about Agrippina, the one where Nietzsche got into trouble and Scheler was quite at home). This fellow-sharer in our national destiny, a pimp by the name of Schmenz, always seized on my shoes and boots in frantic gratitude, washed my shirts and socks for me, sewed on my buttons, ironed my trousers—because my ardent letters evoked rapturous responses in the recipients. The letters were on a very high plane, almost esoteric, markedly stylized, and in that milieu this kind of thing is as popular as a permanent wave. Once Schmenz even gave me half his share of the caramel pudding with which our Sundays used to be enhanced, and for a long time I imagined he did not like caramel pudding (pimps are the fussiest kind of people I have ever had anything to do with), until I later received convincing proof that caramel pudding was one of his favorite dishes. As word soon got round that I knew how to write ardent letters, I soon, less from necessity than by force, built up a clientele as a letter-composer if not actually as an author. Fees usually consisted of strange favors: *not* to pinch tobacco from my locker and meat from my plate, *not* to push me into the muddy ditch when we took our morning exercise, not to trip me up during night marches, and various other favors which exist among such fellow-sharers in national destiny. Some of my friends, Marxists and anti-Marxists, have since accused me of wrongful behavior in the writing of these love letters. It was my duty, they said, "to allow this pent-up ardor to bring about a change of awareness in these illiterate persons, resulting possibly in a revolt," and it was my duty as an upright man to look around for support every morning in the muddy ditch. I am ashamed to admit that I did indeed act wrongly, and was inconsistent, for two totally unrelated reasons, of which the first is a congenital and the second an environmental defect: courtesy, and fear of getting beaten up. Actually I would have been happier if Schmenz had not cleaned my boots and the others had gone on pushing me into the ditch or dunking my cigarette paper in my breakfast coffee, but I lacked both the discourtesy and the courage to prevent them granting me these favors. I blame myself, I acknowledge that it is entirely my fault, and now perhaps the hands which were about to be wrung in despair will fall, the furrowed brows will become smooth again, and here and there someone will wipe the foam from the corners of his mouth. I solemnly promise that at the end of this work I will make a full confession and offer a ready-made moral, as well as an interpretation which will spare all interpreters, from high school student to university professor, the trouble of sighing and wondering.

It will be presented in such a way that even the unsophisticated reader can "digest it," not nearly as involved as the directions on how to complete an application for an income tax refund. Patience, patience, we're not there yet. I must confess that, in our free, pluralistic, industrial society, I naturally prefer a free shoeshine man with a lordly contempt for tips.

Let us now leave me to myself for a few minutes, with my dirty nails, my well-polished shoes, in Streetcar Number 7. Endearing and old-fashioned (nowadays streetcars are nothing but machines for bundling people in and out), the Number 7 wobbles around the east nave of the Cathedral, swings into Unter-Taschenmacher-Strasse in the direction of the Altermarkt, is already approaching the Heumarkt, and no sooner than the Malzmühle but no later than the curve by the Malzbüchel, where I always used to jump off, I shall have to make up my mind whether to go home first and console my father (or my parents. My father's telegram, "Mother passed away," to which I owed my temporary release from this compulsory mutual fellowship, might easily have been a bluff. My mother would have been quite capable of feigning death), or whether I should go right on to the Perlengraben and visit the Bechtolds first. We will leave this question unanswered for the moment, till the streetcar reaches the Malzmühle, and turn back to the ordure section of that sharers-in-our-national-destiny camp where I first met Engelbert Bechtold, from now on to be called, like every Engelbert in Cologne: Angel. That's what he was known as at home, in camp, by me, and that's what he looked like.

The fervent desire of that superior officer whom I had struck in the back of the knee during spade drill with the sharp edge of my spade (and I did not plan it that way, as my Marxist and other friends would have it: on the contrary—a confession that will fill them and everyone else with despair—I was impelled by an invisible and celestial common sense)—the fervent desire of that superior to make a man of me had banished me with all possible speed to those fields where Angel, a mythical figure in the camp, had for three months been steadily and steadfastly pursuing the most varied assortment of dirty jobs: every day he had to empty the huge latrine, which was not connected with the sewer (I will spare myself and the reader the statistical details), he had to empty the kitchen garbage into pig buckets, clean out and light the stoves in the officers' mess, fill the coal scuttles, remove the traces of their carousings (consisting mainly of vomited potato salad mixed with beer and liquor), and look through the mountainous supply of potatoes in the cellar for rotten potatoes to prevent the spread of decay.

The moment I came face to face with Angel I knew

that what had sent me here to make a man of me had not been my own volition, still less something as absurd as a plan, nor my superior's curses, but, as I say, that invisible power of celestial common sense. When I saw Angel I also knew: If he had to perform any kind of duty at all, it was bound to be carrying ordure, and it was an honor for me to do likewise in his company.

Wherever people are forced to become sharers in national destiny, the noble state of manhood is conferred not by advantage but by disadvantage. (Patience: I am well aware of how disadvantage can be turned into advantage and will watch out accordingly.) I still regard my Chopin tour of official duty as something of a black mark against me, although my comparative youth—I was twenty-two—may help to exonerate me. Other advantages (which were not "transformed disadvantages" but genuine advantages), I do not regard as black marks—for instance, that in my capacity of battalion coal heaver—it will be seen from this that I did not carry *only* ordure—I conducted involved and, for reasons of sublimated eroticism, protracted negotiations with the mother superior of a Benedictine convent of the Eternal Adoration in a little town near Rouen, lengthy conversations lasting for over a week (I had, among other things, to allay her fears that I might be a *provocateur*), in order to get permission for two baths a week in exchange for the coal she so desperately needed for the convent laundry. Between us, she and I worked out an advanced mathematical system of diplomacy and eroticism, under the patronage of Pascal and Péguy. And although the nuns knew my church affiliation to be obscure, they invited me to a special service on Assumption Day, entertaining me afterwards with tea and streusel cake (the mother superior was aware of my dislike of coffee). I chivalrously returned the honor with an extra hundredweight of coal and three snow-white officer's handkerchiefs which I had stolen with my own hands—I was especially proud of this feat—from a German Army depot and which at my own expense had been embroidered by a crippled schoolteacher with the words: "Make to yourselves friends of the mammon of unrighteousness. Votre ami allemand." It would complicate this work unnecessarily were I to enumerate other, let alone all, advantages which I enjoyed, for instance: that a very pretty Rumanian Jewish girl in a dry goods shop in Jassy kissed me on both cheeks, mouth and forehead, with the strange remark, murmured in Yiddish: "Because you belong to such a poor people"—the affair had a prologue and an epilogue, I am merely giving the central section because the rest would be too hard to explain. As for a Hungarian colonel who assisted me in falsifying a document, I shall not even begin to go into that.

Let us quickly double back, first to Streetcar Number 7, which has just passed the Malzmühle and is toiling protestingly up the Mühlenbach toward the Waidmarkt—then back to the ordure section in the camp where I suddenly found myself face to face with Angel, who was sitting on a ledge between the kitchen, the sick bay and the latrine having his lunch: a piece of dry bread, a cigarette he had rolled himself, a mug of ersatz coffee. The way he was sitting there reminded me of the streetcleaners at home, whose dignified style of lunch while they sat beside the Tauzieher monument I had always admired and always envied. Angel, like all Lochner's angels, had fair, almost golden hair, he was short and stocky, and although his features—a broad nose, mouth too small, an almost uncannily high forehead—had nothing classical about them, they seemed radiant. In his dark eyes not a trace of melancholy. When I stopped in front of him, he said: "Morning," nodded as if we had arranged to meet there four hundred years ago and I was a trifle late, and said, without putting down his coffee mug: "You should marry my sister"; setting his mug down on the ledge he added: "She's a pretty girl, although she looks like me. She's called Hildegard."

I was silent, as only a man can be silent who has received an angel's annunciation and command. Angel stubbed out his cigarette on the wall, put the butt into his pocket, picked up the two empty lard pails, and proceeded to give me some practical instructions on my impending occupation, mainly scientific details as to how much would go into a ladle, measured in kilos, the load capacity of the pole the ladle was attached to. He threw in a few chemical details but refrained from mentioning the hygienic aspects, no doubt because there was a large sign over the latrine saying: "Bowel movement over, meal time ahead,/ Hands should be washed before you are fed!" It will be observed that those who pack their children off to the army right away need not be afraid the army will overlook anything. If one bears in mind that there is a sign in the mess hall saying: "Work makes us free," it will immediately be seen that the army takes as much thought for poetry as for a man's ethical views.

I spent only two weeks working with Angel at the duties which still enable me to earn my living any day as a sewer worker or a potato sorter. Never again have I seen so many potatoes at any one time as were stored in that cellar under the kitchen: daylight fell dimly through tiny slits onto enormous brown piles that seemed to heave like a seething swamp, sickly alcoholic vapors filled the cellar when we had finished sorting a great heap of rotten potatoes and set them aside to be carried away. The positive side of our labors consisted in carrying the precious fruit upstairs in buckets (I might add, for the peace of mind of all mothers, in *different* buckets) into the kitchen, where it was tipped into the tubs which had been set up for the communal evening potato-peeling.

When we brought the first buckets up into the kitchen, the first thing we were given was what the kitchen supervisor (one of the few people in this compulsory mutual fellowship with no previous conviction) called the snail's blessing, i.e.: we had to throw ourselves down on the greasy dirty floor and crawl right round the huge stove, we were only allowed to raise our heads above the floor just far enough to keep from scraping our faces. The only way we were allowed to help propel ourselves along was to push with our toes; if we used our hands or knees, or stopped moving from exhaustion, our punishment was having to sing, and we were ordered to do this with the words: "A song, a merry song!" and to this day I am not sure whether it was sheer inspiration or whether there was some unconscious rapport between Angel and myself: in any case, the very first time I immediately began singing the song that seems to have been part of Angel's repertoire: *"Deutschland, Deutschland über alles."* It is to be observed that, while they were making men of us, the patriotic side of our feelings was not neglected either, and anyone who is afraid his sons might ever forget they were Germans should pack them off to the army with even greater dispatch than was proposed on Page 19, in the hope that they receive the toughest possible training. Like the conscientious person I have always been, I wondered while I sang whether our song could really be called merry. Incidentally, the method described here— I offer this as an advance on my promised interpretation—is the best and most effective one for drilling a young man's nationality or racial origin into him in a manner he will never forget. I recommend it also for the Swiss, the French, and other nations. For not everyone has the good fortune to be kissed by pretty Jewish girls in Rumanian shops.

It will surprise no one to learn that we were too worn out to sing consistently with the perfection customary among choral societies. We simply mumbled the unforgettable and unforgotten text in a kind of singsong chant into the sticky tiled floor. Later on they forbade me—me, of all people!—to sing the Deutschland song, after our camp commandant looked me up one day in the potato cellar, bawled me out for not having a baptism certificate, and, unexpectedly—whether unjustifiably or not, I still don't know, the matter was never cleared up—bellowed the words "lousy Jew" at me, which I have always regarded as a kind of baptism or circumcision. After that I was no longer allowed to sing the Deutschland song, instead I sang the song about the Lorelei.

It will also surprise no one to learn that Angel and I hardly spoke any more, and not at all about Hildegard. We were usually so exhausted by nine-thirty in the morning that we went staggering about our various duties, vomiting from fatigue and nausea. As a result, our sole means of communication was nodding or shaking our heads. Moreover, our vomiting, headaches and fatigue made us more aware of how little chance there was of our disadvantages turning into advantages. When Angel shrugged his shoulders in a certain way— half apologetic, half submissive—I knew he was going to sit down on a pile of potato sacks and say his rosary ("I promised my mother I would").

Needless to say, in this compulsory mutual fellowship there were also "off-duty regular guys," and even an "on-duty" variety in the person of a young officer, a former Protestant theology student of noble bearing who sometimes approached us to "strike up a conversation." I always had a special blend of rotten potatoes and ordure ready for this man, and I would empty it all round me while Angel with his Christian humility actually "got into conversation" with him and—about twice during those two weeks, each time for three minutes—

humbly accepted words like "necessity," "spirit of the age," "destiny," the way a beggar accepts a slice of dry bread.

By now the Number 7 was not far from the Waidmarkt, and all I could think about was Hildegard Bechtold. There had been times during the past two weeks when I had planned to just go ahead and write her a letter "asking for her hand" (in those days I knew of no other way of putting it, and I still know of no better), but just at this time my evening letter clients were pressing me inordinately, threatening me because they were beginning to find my vocabulary too "refined" after all. The crude endearments which my clients wished to convey to their partners (both primary and secondary sex organs were combined, and these combinations in turn combined with various other physical attributes), were shifted by me onto a still more elevated plane and developed into a mannerist style that still enables me to write letters from every sort of male correspondent to every sort of female recipient which would pass any censorship without suppressing a single thing. In other words, I could earn my living any day as a letter composer. Inasmuch as I have always liked using the blackest possible ink or the softest possible pencil to write on the whitest possible paper, I include my letter composing among the advantages of which I am not ashamed.

By the time we reached the Waidmarkt my anxiety was verging on trepidation, barely another minute and I would be getting out at the Perlengraben. The decision was made. (My mother was dead, that I knew.) Since here, too, on the platform of Number 7, the belt of ordure odor kept me a prisoner in my ivory tower, I perceived what is known as one's environment with the dream-like indistinctness (or distinctness) obtained by looking through high prison windows. A member of the S.A. (how could anyone wear a uniform like that!), a man wearing a silk tie (obviously an upper-class type), a girl eating grapes with innocent fingers out of a paper bag, and the conductress, the beauty of whose young, slightly coarse features was enhanced by that frank eroticism which used to be the mark of Cologne streetcar conductresses—they all avoided me like the plague. I pushed my way through to the exit, jumped off, raced along the Perlengraben, and three minutes later was climbing the stairs to the fourth floor of a block of cheap flats. To the interpreter seeking for reality, I suggest he draw a semicircle of three minutes radius west of Severin-Strasse from the Perlengraben streetcar stop, and choose one of the streets caught in his semicircle—of course, in order to give the radius correctly I ought also to state my speed: I suggest any speed between Jesse Owens and an above-average amateur. I was not surprised to see a transparency over the Bechtolds' front door with the words: "Behold him! Who? The bridegroom. Behold him! How? As he were a lamb." Just as I was about to press the bell—it is hardly necessary to mention this, but it is better to be on the safe side—Hildegard opened the door, fell into my arms, and all my bad odor was taken from me.

III

It is neither my purpose nor within the scope of my capabilities even to try and describe, let alone explain, the power of love. One thing is certain: it was not love at first sight. It was not till an hour later, when I had survived the initiation rites of the Bechtold clan, the betrothal coffee had been drunk and the betrothal cake half consumed, that I got around to having a proper look at Hildegard. I found her much more beautiful than her resemblance to Angel might have led one to expect, and this was a relief. Although I had been in love with her for two weeks, it was nice to find she was beautiful. If I say that from now on we, Hildegard and I, em-

braced, not very often but as often as we could, and if I
say again that I attribute this to the guidance of that
celestial common sense which inspired me, at the words
"Down spades," suddenly to forget everything I had
ever learned, I am afraid that parents who are worried
about their sons will now consider packing them off to
the army not only for educational purposes but also in
the hope that, by the roundabout means of doing the
wrong thing at the command "Down rifles" (for of
course they don't use spades nowadays), they may win
a wife as wonderful, clever and beautiful as mine. So I
would like to warn the reader, by reminding him of
various relevant fairy tales, that the person who unin-
tentionally does good reaps a richer reward than the
person who intentionally imitates him, and I would like
to reiterate: I did not do it intentionally. (I will leave
room here for the gnashing teeth of those angry people
who, intoxicated with intentions as they unfortunately
are, refuse to admit that a celestial common sense can
work to the benefit of those who have no intentions at
all.) Needless to say, I am not acquainted with all the
intentions of that guiding common sense: undoubtedly
one of them was that the Bechtold family be kept supplied with coffee not only for the duration of the war
but as long as they lived (my father owned a wholesale
coffee business, which I have meanwhile inherited). A
secondary intention: to bring to my notice, in the form

of my two brothers-in-law, that diabolism of the twenties of which until September 22, 1938, I had no inkling (child of middle-class parents, graduated from high school, one semester under Ernst Bertram, not yet a member of either National Socialist or any other organizations). Possible further intentions: to give me, at the moment of my mother's death, my mother-in-law (she would have been capable not only of feigning death: later, in her forthright fashion, she even forced her way up to the area commander and called him a "feebleminded, pigheaded, idiotic thing" because on one occasion he refused to extend my leave, when my little daughter had scarlet fever). Additional intentions: to provide my father, in the person of old Mr. Bechtold, with someone to talk to for the rest of his life, someone with whom he could grumble about the Nazis; and to use my cigarette coupons to keep Angel's youngest brother Johann, an inveterate smoker, in cigarettes throughout the tobacco-rationing period— i.e., nearly eleven years. It is possible that this guiding common sense also had an economic balance in mind: we had money, the Bechtolds did not. The coffee is the only thing I am sure about: in the times we knew were in store for us, no family would have been so completely at a loss without coffee as the Bechtolds. At the slightest excuse every single member of the family would ask: "Shall I put on some more coffee?" Although one could

be sure at any given time that four or five pots of coffee
had already been made. Later on, when war actually
broke out, I committed two cardinal sins at once: I in-
dulged in both statistics and psychology—I reduced
the Bechtold family's consumption of coffee from some
two hundred pounds a year to seventy-five, estimating
that the war would last seven years (whether out of
pessimism or a mystical passion for the number seven I
don't know), and persuaded my father to lay in stocks
of raw coffee accordingly. And I goaded my mother-in-
law into economizing on coffee, conjuring up before her
horrified eyes the vision of a coffeeless era if she failed
to economize.

IV

Before I continue I wish to give solemn assurance that
from now on the subject of ordure is as closed as
Chopin was back on Page 9. I have also come to the end
of my portrayal of training methods in military estab-
lishments. The suspicion might be too easily aroused
that this work is anti-militarist or even pro-disarmament
or anti-armament. Oh no, I am concerned with something much more exalted, with—as every unprejudiced

reader is already aware—with <u>love and innocence</u>. The fact that the circumstances under and the details with which I am now attempting to depict these things necessitate the mention of certain formations, organizations and institutions, is not my fault but the fault of a destiny with which anyone may quarrel to his heart's content. It is not my fault that I write in German, that in the potato cellar of a German fellowship of national destiny I was made a Jew by the commandant bellowing at me, that in the back room of a cheap Rumanian shop I was made a German by a pretty Jewish girl kissing me. Had I been born in Ballaghaderreen I would be writing—with the darkest possible ink or the softest possible pencils on the whitest possible paper—about love and innocence under quite different circumstances and with quite different details. I would be singing about dogs and horses and donkeys, about fair maidens I kissed behind the hedge after a dance, to whom I had promised what I intended to keep but then could not keep: marriage. I would sing of the moors, the bog, the wind whining in the peat ditches, whipping up dark water in the peat ditches and making them billow like the dark tweed skirt of a maiden who has drowned herself because the one who kissed her and promised to marry her became a priest and went his way. I would fill many pages to sing the praises of the dogs of Dukinella; those clever faithful beasts, thoroughbreds and mongrels alike, have long deserved a monument in words. But, things being what they are, I sharpen my pencil again, not to relate anything unpleasant but to tell what happened—so let us return with a sigh to Cologne, to that street to be found inside a western semicircle of three minutes around the Perlengraben, if it is to be found at all. It has not been swallowed up by the ground, it has been swept away, scraped away, and in order not to leave this page in the coloring book completely blank, thus opening wide the gates to nonsense, I offer three small landmarks: a tobacco shop, a fur store, a school, and a number of yellowish-white house fronts, almost the same color, though not the same size, as the ones I saw in Pilsen. I suggest that intelligent and obedient art students draw three steamshovels, one carrying away the fur store, one the tobacco shop, and one the school, and that they write across the top of the page the motto: "Work makes us free."

The trouble is, though, that no one will know where to hang the plaque when one day Angel acquires the odor of sanctity. I don't have to be told that I cannot represent the Congregation of Rites, or raise the question of canonization without a devil's advocate, but, inasmuch as my church affiliation is obscure, it will not, I hope, hurt anyone's feelings if I procure a saint for a church to which I probably do not belong. Like everything else in this work, it is not done deliberately. Naturally the fact that Angel has been both matchmaker and brother-in-law to me is enough to make uncharitable people say "Aha," but may I not, since the column "church affiliation" has to remain blank, at least point out that I spent two weeks with Angel and therefore use a little of the odor of sanctity to chase away the odor of ordure from these pages? I can see I shall have no such luck, I am suspected of ulterior motives. Never mind, I won't bother, if only because courtesy (so they say) is not a theological category. Besides, my father is still alive, has long ceased to go to alternate churches, he doesn't go to church at all, won't let me see his tax return, still grumbles about the Nazis with old Mr. Bechtold, my father-in-law.

The two of them are now completely absorbed in a new interest: exploring the layers of Cologne. They dig away in a shaft my father has had sunk in our courtyard and roofed over, and they assure us plausibly, although with a good deal of snickering, that they have discovered the remains of a temple of Venus. My mother-in-law is in her charming way a Catholic, like the Cologne motto: "We are the ones who decide whether something is Catholic or not." When I am forced to discuss religious matters with her (I am the father of a twenty-four-year-old daughter, who at the fervent wish of my deceased wife was brought up a Catholic, then married a Protestant, becoming in turn the mother of a thirteen-year-old daughter who at her fervent wish is being brought up a Catholic), and present convincing evidence that her view does not coincide with the official one of her church, she dismisses this with a pronouncement I hesitate to repeat: "Then all I can say is, the Pope was wrong." And when—as is sometimes unavoidable—there are church dignitaries present who contradict her personal brand of Papism, she refuses to budge and relies on a statement which it is as impossible to prove as it is to refute: "We Kerkhoffs (her maiden name was Kerkhoff) have always been Catholics by instinct." It is not up to me to dissuade her of this. I am too fond of her. To augment the confusion about this kind soul (who once during the war threw, literally threw, a military policeman—who was searching for her deserter son, Anton—down the stairs single-handed), let me add the following touch for the coloring book: that for six weeks she was the leader of a Communist Party cell, till she realized that "this business" was incompatible with her instinctive Catholicism, and she was also, and is still, chairman of a Rosary Fellowship.

As a background for at least one of the pages to be devoted to her in the coloring book, I suggest a blue which anyone who has ever painted the sky above Naples is sure to have. If the reader now "hasn't the slightest idea what to make of her," I have achieved my object, and now everyone may take their crayons, paintbox or palette and color my mother-in-law whatever color seems to convey "dubious" or "scandalous." I suggest a soft mauve shading to red. I shall not have a great deal more to say about my mother-in-law, I value her too much to expose her to the light, I am keeping the greater part of her to myself in my private darkroom. I will gladly reveal a few of her external features: she is short, was at one time slim but now "has put on a lot of weight," she still drinks staggering quantities of coffee; at an advanced age, seventy-two, she has become a confirmed smoker and occupies herself with her grandchildren "quite outrageously": the children of my deceased brother-in-law Anton, who was "a declared atheist and an out-and-out Leftist," two girls between eighteen and twenty-one, she drags off to the kitchen, says the rosary with them, and goes through the Creed; the children of my surviving brother-in-law Johann (a boy and girl, ten and twelve), who are being brought up in strict observance of church discipline, she is "injecting with obstinacy and rebellion." (All the quotation marks denote her own words.)

For her I am still "that nice boy who made my Hilde so happy and who for months on end (it was actually only two weeks) carried shit with my Angel." (Once again I am forced, in the interest of historical ac-

curacy, to utter the blunt word.) She has no more forgotten these two facts than that "he kept me supplied
with coffee in war and peace." It is perhaps to her
credit that she always mentions my material services
last. But otherwise she considers me "terribly naïve," if
only for the fact that I was "witless enough to let them
shoot at him, and even hit him."

This is something she cannot understand. She feels
that "any intelligent person, who really and truly had
nothing to do with that business (in this case she means
the Nazi business), ought to have been able to avoid it."
She is probably right, and when I begin arguing with
her and remind her how Angel died, she will say: "You
know perfectly well that Angel was not intelligent, or
that he was more than that," and there she is right. I
don't know why I actually allowed myself to be shot at,
what's more to be hit, or why, although I was "exempt
from shooting," I exposed myself to the line of fire
without doing any shooting myself. It remains a stain
on my consciousness and my conscience. Probably I was
just tired of listening to Chopin; or perhaps I was just
tired of the West and longed for the East; I don't quite
know what it was that caused me simply to ignore the
certificate of the consulting ophthalmologist of the
Western Army division. Hildegard wrote me at the time
that she understood, but I didn't understand myself.
My mother-in-law is right to associate the word witless

with my behavior then and now. It remains totally obscure, dark, and I authorize anyone to take some black ink and a piece of cotton and dab a nice big blot onto the coloring book just where my consciousness should be. In any event, I had given up the idea of deserting, I saw nothing attractive about exchanging my present captivity for any other. "What kind of music do the Russians play on the piano?" asked my mother-in-law when I came home on leave from the front. I told her what was true, that I had only heard the piano played a few times, and it had always been Beethoven. "That's good," she said, "that's very good."

Here, in the midst of our idyll, I wish to perform a neglected duty and propose a page or two for the erection of a memorial niche where I shall fill in only the commemorative tablets for those persons in this work who are now dead.

1. Hildegard Schmölder, née Bechtold, born January 6, 1920, died May 31, 1942, during an air raid on Cologne in a street in the vicinity of Clovis Square. Her mortal remains were never found.

2. Engelbert Bechtold, known as Angel, born September 15, 1917, shot on December 30, 1939, between

Forbach and St. Avold by a French sentry who must have thought he was going to attack, although all he wanted to do was to give himself up. His mortal remains were never found.

3. Anton Bechtold, born May 12, 1915, executed one day in February 1945 behind the terrace of the Café Reichard in Cologne, between what are now the headquarters of the radio station and the cathedral residences, not far from the tourist bureau, "just opposite the cathedral," where today unsuspecting tourists and still more unsuspecting radio producers sip their iced coffee. Although his mortal remains were never found, his dossier was. He was listed as having "deserted twice," accused of stealing from and black-marketing in army supplies, and of organizing a group of deserters in the cellars of bombed-out houses in the Old Town and staging regular battles against the "police units of the German Wehrmacht." His widow, Monika Bechtold, used to talk a lot about "it," now she doesn't talk about "it" any more.

I offer this little funeral chapel in the midst of our idyll unadorned, just the bare brickwork, so to speak. Anyone is free to follow his bent or taste and decorate it with dog roses, pansies or privet. Even roses are allowed, prayers may be said, and there is no objection to meditating on the transitoriness of man's mortal self. And I ask those who wish to pray not to forget Anton:

I never liked him, but, when the trumpets sound on the Day of Judgment, I wish him a kiss from the gentlest of all the angels of Judgment, from an auxiliary angel who is not entitled to blow trumpets, just to polish them. I wish Anton redemption from his simulated wickedness, from his failure to be understood and his failure to understand. May the angel give him back what even he must once have had: innocence.

V

This more or less exhausts the topic of war too, at least for the duration of this work, and we return to the deep, too deep peace of that September afternoon when I kissed Hildegard for the first time and all my bad odor was suddenly taken from me.

What the Bechtolds called their hallway was an unlighted rectangle about nine feet square with five doors leading off it: three to bedrooms, one to the kitchen, one to the bathroom. Clothes hooks had been hammered directly into the narrow strips of wall between the doors. Dresses, coats, jackets, scarves, shabby dressing gowns and "Mother's funny hats" dangled from them, and a number of these things were always getting caught in

doors as they opened and had to be shoved aside, sometimes from the inside, which led to hands getting
caught.

At the very moment when I was embracing Hildegard, three doors opened: Mrs. Bechtold came out of
the kitchen, Mr. Bechtold out of the bedroom, Anton
and Johann out of their room, and all four struck up
the hymn—Hilde, the fifth, wept in silent bliss against
my chest—"Behold him! How? As he were a lamb."

By this time, if not before, the astute reader will
know what we—he and I—ought no longer to withhold
from the less astute reader: namely, that this work is
really designed as an idyll pure and simple, to fulfill the
same function among the aromas of sewage as elsewhere
the perfume of roses, by avoiding or at least greatly
reducing the necessity of dealing with the war, and dis-
missing the Nazi business as something between a cold
and a hail of brimstone; and although on a later page
Angel and I, despite our geographical separation, became Stormtroopers and joined the S.A. simultaneously
(even if only fictitiously, for we did our service elsewhere
and never wore the terrible S.A. uniform) everyone
knows that I would have done better to be born in Ballaghaderreen and chosen a lyre rather than the crest of Cologne as a watermark for my letter paper. I am a German to no purpose, a native of Cologne to no avail, and
when I confess that after the war I took over my fa-

ther's coffee business and now steadfastly refuse to be
either shocked or concerned over the fact that last
year's turnover has risen 3.7 per cent less than the
turnover of the preceding year, which rose 4.9 per cent
as compared with that of the year before that, it will
become apparent that my brothers-in-law were justified
in referring to me as "Buttercup." In vain do I try to
soothe my manager with bonuses. He understands
neither my allusions to the fiery chariot that carried
Elijah off to heaven, nor the fact that I allow my three-
year-old granddaughter to play with our complicated
and costly accounting machines; and when I let the
Income Tax Department look after the repair bills he is
indignant, shocked, just as he is at the fact that I refer
to these achievements of science as a mere improvement
on the loom. His fear that the business is going "down-
hill" does not alarm me. Where else should it go? When
I walk down to the Leystapel by the river and along the
Frankenwerft, I have to restrain myself from plunging
into the dark waters of the Rhine. Only my granddaughter's hand holds me back, and the thought of my
mother-in-law. I am a tea drinker, so why should I
worry about the coffee business?

My father and father-in-law do not hold me back.
Their age has carried them over a new threshold of
pleasure, as old as the rubble they burrow in. They have
"become one with Cologne," and it is vanished potency,

not wisdom, that prevents them from crowning their snickering voluptuousness with the joys of Venus. Old man Bechtold, whose proletarian bravura used to impress me, has become quite soigné, and when the two old men climb up out of their shaft and bring to light a stone or a fragment of scribbled pottery, it is not only their panting tongues that remind me of dogs. Their snickering adds to my suspicion that all we have been is bait: Angel, Hildegard, myself, each of us bait for the other—and in the background there must have always been someone snickering. Whatever happened to us or whatever we did always suited someone: whether we weighed coffee, carried ordure, let ourselves be shot at, lived or died. My mother's death suited many people extremely well: the Bechtolds, me, even my father, who "couldn't bear to go on watching her suffer"; even herself, she couldn't stand the dreadful faces and the uniforms, she was not religious and not innocent, not sophisticated and not sufficiently corrupted to live in a sewer. The Protestant pastor's words at her graveside were so embarrassing that I prefer not to repeat them. There are certain manifestations of hypocrisy that I pass over with celestial courtesy. When the trumpets sound on the Day of Judgment, I hope the angels will not take all the words he ever spoke during his lifetime and stuff them back into his mouth like a mountain of candy floss.

When he expressed his condolences to my father and me after the funeral, he looked disapprovingly at my civilian clothes and whispered severely: "Why aren't you wearing your country's uniform?" and because of this remark I herewith dub him the most unpleasant character in this work, infinitely more unpleasant than the officer who gave us the snail's blessing while wearing his country's uniform. Silently I held out my dirty nails to the pastor, as we used to at inspection. This is the only deliberate impertinence I can boast of. Twenty years later I saw him again as my son-in-law's uncle at my daughter's wedding, I held out my—this time clean—nails to him, and that was not a deliberate impertinence but merely, as every psychologist knows, a reflex movement. He went scarlet, stammered when he started talking again, refused our invitation to the wedding reception, and my son-in-law is still angry with me for having ruined "the harmony of the day."

I hope these flashes back and forth will not upset the reader. By grade 7, if not before, the merest child knows that this is called changing the narrational level. It is the same thing as change of shift in a factory, except that in my case these changes mark the places where I have to sharpen my pencil before supplying more strokes and dots. Here I am seen at the age of twenty-one, twenty-three, I shall appear at the age of twenty, and then not until I am almost fifty. I am seen as a bridegroom, as a husband, then not again until I am a widower and a grandfather—nearly twenty years are blank pages for which I shall supply a few decorative outlines but no contents. Let us hurry back with freshly sharpened pencil to the level "Afternoon of September 22, 1938, about quarter past five."

VI

The song of welcome has died away, I feel Hildegard's tears damp on my neck and cheeks, a few of her long hairs lie, golden as the hair of Lochner's angels, on my white shirt. From the open kitchen door comes the smell of fresh coffee—who is going to make tea for me in this house?—freshly baked Rodons (elsewhere known as Gugelhupf cake). Through the open bedroom door I can see Anton Bechtold's easel, on which a chaotic painting done entirely in purples and yellows explicitly (for my taste *too* explicitly) represents a naked woman reclining on a purple couch. Through the other open door I can see a whole pile of leather, some eighteen by thirty inches square, reddish yellow, a cobbler's stool, and a still burning cigar lying in an enormous ashtray made to look like a pond with swans. After unsuccessful

settlement proceedings and a successful, but not fraud-
ulent, bankruptcy, old Mr. Bechtold had to shut down
his shoemaker's business, and he now had a modest shoe-
repair shop in the living room, as well as earning "you
can't call it a living, let's just say an existence" (quotation from my mother-in-law) as a leather salesman.

An embarrassed silence follows, to be expected, no
doubt, after a miracle. Should anyone wish to ask at
this point: "How did the Bechtolds know you were coming, and even if they knew your mother had died—what
exactly did she die of, anyway?—how could Engelbert
let you know so fast that they could prepare such a
wonderful welcome for you?" the only honest reply I
can give is that shrug of the shoulders a person gives
who hasn't the faintest idea of the answer and with
which I have reduced many a questioner to despair.
And when I go on to add that our camp of fellow-
sharers in national destiny was situated more than 200
miles from Cologne, in the heart of the forest from
which came most of Grimms' fairy tales, that Angel was
permanently confined to barracks, that, although the
Bechtolds must have known I was coming, they were
demonstrably unaware that my mother had died—I can
only point to angelic messengers or the tom-tom as a
source of news; *I* at any rate know no other explanation
—and in the midst of this embarrassed silence old man
Bechtold said to his sons, with a motion of his head I

found quite uncanny (it reminded me of a myrmidon's
nod) : "You might as well settle it with him right
away." I was torn from Hildegard's arms and led off in
the direction of the easel, a door was slammed shut behind me. I saw two untidy beds, two dressers, a book-
shelf with suspiciously few books (some seven to ten),
but a lot of painting gear, also a dozen or so fresh
canvases of Anton's all based on a series of sins ("Sin
among the Middle Classes," "Sin among the Lower
Middle Classes," "Sin in the Proletariat," "Sin in the
Church," etc.)

I was made to sit down on a wooden chest, Johann
pressed a leather dice box into my hand and told me "to
try my luck on the floor." I shook the dice box, turned
it upside down on the floor—although it was my first
and last dice game, Anton and Johann nodded ap-
proval at my technique. I threw two fives and a six,
which made Johann flip his cigarette into the air in
fury and shout "Oh shit!" (I quote). Here I must add
that these two male Bechtolds, unlike Angel and their
father, were dark-haired, short and tough, and wore
little Mephistophelean mustaches. When after they had
both thrown pitiful twos and threes, I shyly asked what
the stake was, they indicated dumbly that I was to
throw again, and this time I threw two fives and a four,
which provoked them both to such lurid utterances that
I shall pass over them with the same celestial courtesy

as over the pastor's hypocrisy. I find certain forms of
male frankness in sexual terminology as suspect as
candy floss, unless they have a place in professional jargon—pimps', for example. Perhaps my association with
pimps had made me rather choosy in this respect, sensitive to style: anyway, I did not blush, which is what the
other two had evidently expected. I started to sweat, I
felt the bad odor suddenly cling to me again, but it was
not till I had won the third round by an easy margin
that it dawned on me what the stake was: which of the
three Bechtold brothers was to make the sacrifice of
joining the S.A. They had picked me to shake the dice
box in Angel's place. One of old man Bechtold's former
schoolmates, who among other things was in charge of
supplying leather to the S.A. units of Cologne South,
West and North, had hinted that Bechtold could
"count on a sizeable order if at least one of your sons
decides to join our ranks." That despite my mother-in-
law's protests one of them did join, that despite my
victorious throws it was Angel who applied for admission in the S.A., and I did not want him to be there all
by himself so I applied for admission at the same time
as he did; that we both had the misfortune to be accepted although our commanding officer issued a very
bad report on us, I couldn't even produce a baptism
certificate—to elaborate on such complicated proce-
dures, let alone render them credible, is beyond me: for

this page in the coloring book I suggest a frenzied pencil scrawl, standing for a stylized dense forest. When I go on to admit that every Christmas, every single year, regardless of where I happened to be (once I spent it in prison), I received a little parcel containing half a pound of Speculatius cookies, three cigarettes, and two chocolate wafers, from the "Stormtroopers' unit, Cologne South," accompanied by a mimeographed letter that started off "To our S.A. comrades at the front" and signed "Thinking of you all, Your Unit Leader," it becomes obvious that I was justly included in the category of exploiters of the system, in spite of the fact that old man Bechtold never got his order and never sold so much as a single ounce of leather to the S.A. It is galling enough to commit acts of stupidity, but it is even more galling to commit them uselessly. However, this confession makes it possible for me to supply a splendid contribution for the pages covering six years of my life: for each page, a little box about three by five inches square.

I must not forget to mention the sole survivor, apart from my father, mother-in-law and father-in-law, from the year 1938: my brother-in-law Johann. After a sinful youth, war actually made a man of him and cleansed him; fully restored to the (Catholic) religion of his fathers, he came home with the rank of infantry sergeant, went to university, got his degree, took up the

respected career of textile merchant (doctor of political
science), and today dismisses his deceased brother as "a
queer fish, a radical Leftist." He regards me with suspicion because the blemish of membership in the S.A.
still clings to me. Naturally I have too much celestial
courtesy to remind him of the dice scene in the bedroom
of my brothers-in-law. I believe if I actually did try to
remind him he would look at me as if I were a liar.

If I fail to mention either my daughter or granddaughter, my son-in-law or mother-in-law, as being still
alive, or even merely alive, it is because I have something else in store for them. In order of my affection I
shall make use of them as keystones in the closing pages
of this idyllic coloring book. I shall chip away at them a
bit and stylize them, to make them fit in and look
decorative.

My mother-in-law's insistence on a speedy wedding
was not a matter of calculation, although she admitted
to me time and again how glad she was to get her
daughter married off so satisfactorily. It was her
anxiety to legalize and sanction something she called
"unmistakable sensuality" and "this forever being together." Furthermore, she confessed quite frankly that
she was afraid of "illegitimate grandchildren or those
born too soon after the wedding." Inasmuch as I was of
age and the photocopying machines were running at

full speed to keep up with the demand for proof of
Aryan origin, and any document was readily obtainable
at low cost (except for my baptism certificate), after a
hasty and depressing funeral (my mother's) there was
a hasty wedding, of which there is even a photo. In this
photo Hildegard looks strangely despondent, and the
faces of my two brothers-in-law show mocking grins. A
civil marriage certificate exists with swastikas and German eagles, in which I am described as an "arts student, at present laborer." Since Hildegard desired our
union to be blessed in church, there is also a church
marriage certificate bearing the stamp of the parish of
St. John the Baptist. A wedding breakfast was held in
the Bechtolds' apartment ("I'm certainly not going to
be done out of that"), a quadrille and a polka were
improvised before we were allowed to withdraw to the
hastily rented furnished room near Clovis Square
(rent, twenty-five marks a month), for a marriage
which was supposed to last about twenty-three hours
but actually lasted nearly a week. Should youthful or
even mature readers regard this period as too short for
a marriage, allow me to point out that many a marriage
that has gone on for twenty years has not lasted a week,
and if the fact that I was arrested, not on the first day
but on the seventh, and taken away to a (different)
compulsory body of mutual fellowship, should arouse
suspicion toward or contempt for the authorities, I

must point to the loyalty of the Bechtold clan and my
father, who stated that we had "left town, destination
unknown." We never discovered who actually betrayed
us. I was arrested in Batteux' dairy in the Severin-
Strasse while, still in my olive-drab trousers and carrying a blue-and-white-striped shopping bag, I was buy-
ing some butter and eggs (rationed now) for our
breakfast (the fresh rolls were already in my shopping
bag), and Hildegard was tidying up our room. Witless,
lost in a kind of blissful timelessness, I mistook the two
fellows in olive-drab uniforms, who suddenly grabbed
my arms, for a bad dream, the cries of the nice sales-
girls at Batteux' for demonstrations of sympathy
(which is what they were). I resisted, shouted abuse
(contrary to my usual practice), and at the subsequent
hearing displayed not only no remorse but something
which was entered in the files rather engagingly as "ob-
stinate pride." The remaining weeks which I should
otherwise have spent among my fellow-sharers in national destiny, I spent in a variety of prisons and dun-
geons, a few days in the Cologne municipal gaol where
I made my written application for admission into the
S.A. Angel I never saw again, and Hildegard not for
nearly two years. We were permitted to exchange a few
censored letters; to my mind a censored letter is not
a letter at all, except as a sign of life. The few
illegal visits Hildegard paid me and I paid her can-

not be called marriage, they were merely assignations.

Meanwhile, equipped now with a proper dossier, I was shifted from one mutual-fellowship camp to another, spent a further five days of marriage in 1940, when my daughter was born, and another two weeks again early in 1941, after I had recovered from the head wound I received from a Frenchman, who had every reason to take me for his enemy: I ran into him as he was hurrying across the road one night with two machine guns which obviously emanated from the armory of the mutual-fellowship camp I was in at the time. In my best mother-superior French I begged him not to put me in a position which might compel me to be discourteous—in what way I had no idea; I suggested he just throw the things down and run away or, for all I cared, run away *with* the things in such a way that, without being discourteous, I could follow him without catching him up, since I was not interested in active combat—but he never let me finish, he shot me in the head with his automatic, left me lying in a pool of blood on the road, and put me in the awkward position of "turning out, much to everyone's surprise, to be a hero," as the commandant of the mutual-fellowship camp later put it. I find this incident highly embarrassing, I only mention it for the sake of literary composition.

This brings me to the end of the topics of war and

marriage, and from now on only the rose perfume of peace shall prevail. Any wartime or postwar elements which, for quantitative reasons, I may be obliged to mention, will be presented in stylized form: either as art nouveau, genre art, or the mannerist style. In any case, they will be transposed back into art-historical periods with picture-postcard appeal. My feelings toward the war are not so much those of the tea drinker toward the coffee business as those of a pedestrian toward motorcars.

VII

As such—as a pedestrian toward motorcars—I now offer some historical material all by itself. I offer it raw, naked, using not my pencil but only my scissors. Let each person do with it or make out of it what he likes: cut out ornaments for his children or paper the walls with it. Nor is the material complete—on the contrary, it is very incomplete; anyone so inclined may stick the pieces together and make a kite and let it sail way up into the air, or he may bend over it with a magnifying glass and count the flyspecks. Magnified or reduced:

the material I offer is genuine; what anyone does with it
is not my business. It might serve as a kind of mourning
edge to be stuck around the pages of the coloring book.
I realized it all at the time, yet it was not real to me—
and so I leave to each reader to form his own reality out
of it.

In Aachen, the first Reich chess tournament was
held, sponsored by the "Strength Through Joy" movement. A player called John used the French defense, a
player called Lehmann the Queen Indian, Zabiensky
the Dutch. A certain Tiltju defeated a certain Rüsken,
who never got moving with his Sicilian defense.

In London a meeting took place between German and
English veterans who expressed their common wish,
their desire, for a *true* peace.

In Berlin there was a convention of animal psychologists. It was declared during this gathering that animal
psychologists were linked to human psychology in
ideals, strife, and work. A Professor Jaensch spoke with
particular emphasis on the psychology of the domestic
chicken and said many problems in human psychology
could be greatly aided by studying the psychology of
the chicken, because the chicken's life perspective, like

the human one, is determined by the sense of sight. The chicken—he said—was the psychologist's pet, while the rabbit might be called the physiologist's pet.

On the same day a convention took place in Berlin on heating and ventilation, in the course of which some principles of ventilation as well as the ventilation regulations of the Standards Association were discussed in detail.

"The time of your life" was promised by a Cologne beer-hall called Zillertal. Millowitsch was appearing in "The Skunk," and the civic theater was doing "The Taming of the Shrew."

In Cologne there was also a meeting that day of thirty-five "Hitler-holidaymakers," who were warmly welcomed by some president or other who pointed out to them that during those days the whole world was looking toward the Rhineland.

Needless to say, the birth rate was declining in Europe.

Comrades of the former 460th Infantry Regiment and the 237th Infantry Division announced their next reunion. In Salzrümpchen at the law school.

As for football, the great question that day was: Will the teams now heading the leagues be able to maintain their position?

A reporter gives a lively account of the progress in the building of the fortifications in the Western part of the Reich:

As we turn the corner, we see the steaming field kitchen coming up the hill toward us drawn by two powerful horses. It smells of sauerkraut and boiled pork.

It is not easy to find a particular place. Everything is so new here. No one here can give any information. The workman knows nothing about the surrounding area. He knows his place of work, he knows the way to his camp. That is all he is interested in. Anyone giving information does so unwillingly and hesitatingly. Everyone displays a healthy distrust.

Everywhere there are camps; we have passed quite a lot of them on our way here, but we want to go to where Dr. Ley was yesterday.

Over there is a fellowship camp in the truest sense of the words. Men from all parts of Germany have gathered together here: from Mecklenburg, from Pomerania, Hamburg, Westphalia, Thüringia, Berlin, and from Cologne a goodly number too. We remember from the war that humor and cheerfulness always prevailed wherever there were men from Cologne in a unit. This is just as true here, but that is not the only reason. The cheerfulness here, says the head cook, is the best sign that the men's stomachs are being well looked after. We have no reason to doubt him, for the leftovers from the midday meal which have been kept for us are very tasty. The Labor Front has the food distribution well in hand, and looks after these things just as well as it does the spiritual needs of the workmen, and one is bound to admit that

EVERYTHING HUMANLY POSSIBLE IS BEING DONE

Each man receives per day: 4 oz. of meat, 28 oz. of potatoes, 8 to 16 oz. of vegetables (according to the variety), 28 oz. of bread, 2 to 3 oz. of butter, 4 oz. of sausage, cheese, etc., as well as chocolate, cigars, ciga- rettes or canned fruit.

The movie truck is in constant use, the camps are provided with radios and libraries, also chess and other indoor games, as well as athletic equipment.

We have seen for ourselves: our Western front stands. These fortifications are being built by Germans. It is the entire German nation which is building its wall of defense here.

With Strength Through Joy through Greece and Yugoslavia. Five ocean giants will cruise to the South during 1938/39. The National Socialist "Strength Through Joy" movement has organized a series of Mediterranean cruises for the coming winter of 1938/39 surpassing all previous programs.

A colonel of the General Staff by the name of Foertsch has published a detailed study of the significance of reserve training. In sober language he gave as his opinion that the *military manpower resources* of a nation lie primarily in its trained reserve units. Certain negative feelings existing temporarily among those recalled for duty would, he said, quickly disappear when people came once again to that realization which on Memorial Day, 1935, had caused the whole nation *with one accord* to breathe a sigh of relief at the reintroduction of conscription. The understanding of the *security needs* of the state and the *nation's spirit of self-sacrifice*, he said, were the two poles governing the extent to which security could be maintained. If an entire generation, he went on, was able for four years to carry on a struggle of indescribable heroism, it was only because for that generation four weeks of reserve duty had not been too much.

The Legal Advice Bureau of the German Labor Front has announced a decision of the Reich Labor Tribunal (No. 154/37) that *refusal to join* the German Labor Front is cause for dismissal without notice. The Legal Advice Bureau concurred with this decision —that such refusal is cause for dismissal without notice, dismissal *with notice* on grounds of nonmembership in the German Labor Front having long been regarded as justifiable; furthermore, dismissal *without notice* is permissible in cases where nonmembership arises from an antisocial attitude.

<u>CUT OUT—KEEP—PIN UP</u>

Every house must be prepared for fire-fighting during air raids and contain at least the minimum air-raid-precaution equipment.

1. As many buckets as possible.

2. Water tub of at least twenty-five gallons capacity.

3. A mop for extinguishing flames and hard-to-reach fire spots. This is to consist of a pole with a piece of cloth on the end to be dipped in water before use.

4. A sandbox with at least two cubic feet of sand or earth and a simple sand shovel (e.g., coal shovel) or

5. Scoops, spades, shovels.

6. Axes and hatchets.

7. Demolition pole (wooden pole with steel hook).

8. Rope (a long, sturdy washing-line).

Most of such items are to be found in the home or can be made at little cost. As soon as the ARP siren is sounded, this equipment is to be placed in the hallways and passages and distributed according to the air-raid warden's instructions.

Weather forecast: Winds southerly, light to moderate, some fog patches in the morning, otherwise sunny, cloudy at times and moderately warm. Further outlook: fair and dry. Due to an interaction of warm subtropical air and mild sea air, there was some precipitation yesterday over northwest France and the English Channel. However, this weak ridge of disturbance was unable to extend its influence appreciably toward the east. On the other hand, owing to a general rise in barometric pressure over western and central Europe, the eastern European high-pressure area was able to advance in a westerly direction. Atmospheric disturbances over the Atlantic which made themselves felt this morning by winds of hurricane force between Ireland and Newfoundland will for the time being have no effect on West Germany. Maximum temperature: 72 degrees; average temperature: 68 degrees; last night's low: 60 degrees. No precipitation.

A sculptor found it necessary to notify the public that an official government emblem showing the German eagle, commissioned by the Army for a military headquarters building, was produced by an old-established firm of art metalworkers—but had been designed by *him*.

To give those readers who are not from the Rhine-land some idea of the mother-poetry of those days, here is a translation from a poem written at that time in the local Cologne dialect:

> Go out into the world, my lad,
> No harm can come to you,
> Mother does not feel too sad,
> Your former comrades, too
>
> Have left their parents' hearth and home,
> And traveled south and west,
> Mother knows you have to roam,
> "My son, you were the best.
>
> What'er betide you, good or ill,
> You never must forget
> That home, sweet home, awaits you still,
> And that I miss you yet."
>
> How brave is such a mother's heart,
> Braver than soldiers all.
> And yet one thing is sure,
> When you're out there and far apart
> Her tears will freely fall.

The announcement that the International Hairdress-ers' Convention was to be held in Cologne, that twenty different nations had agreed to participate, that the first world hairdressing championship was to take place and a contest announced for the challenge trophy donated by Dr. Ley, will fill everyone—at least, all the inhabitants of Cologne—with legitimate pride.

In going on to report some activities of the Bergisch-Gladbach Rabbit Breeders Association, my purpose is not to hold these worthy people up to ridicule. Nor is it for the sake of any literary considerations apropos the above-mentioned convention of animal psychologists: it is based on a certain sense of justice, and especially because some of my friends used to live in this little town. The Bergisch-Gladbach Rabbit Breeders Association announced its annual family outing, which this year was to be a "mystery trip." Friends and supporters were heartily invited to avail themselves of the fun in store for them.

The announcement in the same town of the Veterans' and Home Guard Association's monthly reunion, and the promise of the local branch of the National Socialist "Strength Through Joy" movement of a gay and enjoyable evening, are mentioned here merely for the sake of completeness.

There are a few minor items which I must take care

not to overlook, for, although they are known to "the merest child," there is reason to believe they are not known to the merest grown-up, and so I am taking pains to reiterate what is known to "the merest child":

That in the weeks surrounding September 22, perhaps even on that very day, the discovery was made in the Kaiser Wilhelm Institute in Berlin-Dahlem of that new type of nuclear reaction with which we are all familiar. A few months later, with the caution so characteristic of science, the first research reports were published, and a month after that nuclear physicists all over the world knew that the atom bomb was a technical possibility and that a new era was dawning.

The fact that on that day, September 22, 1938, the Prime Minister of England, Neville Chamberlain, arrived in Bad Godesberg to discuss the so-called Sudeten crisis, is familiar not only to the merest child but virtually to every infant, and I reiterate it now for grownups only. "After Chamberlain," wrote one chronicler of that historic day, "had arrived from Cologne, he looked with evident pleasure out of his window across to the Rhine valley basking in the sunshine, and expressed his complete satisfaction with the choice of this symbolically unrestricted view. He allowed himself to be photographed with that open, friendly smile which his bold flight made world-famous practically overnight."

VIII

My three-year-old granddaughter never calls me
Grandfather, just Wilhelm; when she talks about me to
other people, she says "he has" or "Wilhelm has." So I
am never prepared for it when she asks me about her
grandmother. While we walk along the Leystapel and
the Frankenwerft as far as the Kaiser Friedrich Em-
bankment and back (slowly, I am not too steady on my
legs), I tell her about Anna Bechtold, my mother-in-
law: how she was sent to prison because of her row with
the military police, how she broke out twice, the first
time managed to get as far as Gremberghoven and the
second time as far as Cologne-Deutz, but was caught
both times. I tell it like a folk ballad, letting the bombs
whine as they fall, the shells burst, the M.P.'s appear in
all their martial fierceness. My little granddaughter
Hilde then tugs impatiently at my hand, pointing out
that she wants me to tell her about her grandmother,
not her great-grandmother. I clamber up and down the
genealogical tree till I think I have reached the right
branch and tell her about Katharina Berthen, the
mother of her father (my son-in-law), a person I avoid
as much as possible although she is a beautiful woman,

the same age as I am, and at one time efforts were un-
derway to couple me with her: she reminds me too much
of all my skittish cousins, whose parlor games I still
have lurid memories of, more lurid than the professional
love nest of the lady called Hertha with whom I so often
exchanged letters, although not on my own behalf. The
appalling lassitude of professional vice—after five
years of professional practice it reverts to something
almost like innocence. (Is he really dead? Yes. Did you
see it with your own eyes? Yes. Where? How sad—no
muffled drums. And he was so fond of caramel pudding.) "Of course, the Berthens come from a very old
Cologne family, way back in. . . ." No, she tugs at my
arm with both hands, as if she were pulling on a bell
rope. Grandmother means Hildegard. It is not easy to
imagine that there is someone who thinks of Hildegard
as a grandmother. What can I tell about her? Nothing.
That she was fair and very sweet, that she liked cur-
tains as much as books and geraniums; that at Batteux'
they always gave her more eggs than her ration? Who
can describe innocence? Not me. Who can describe the
happiness and ecstasies of love? Not me. Am I to present Hildegard to my three-year-old granddaughter as
if for inspection: properly washed and naked? No
thanks. Give a detailed account of some three dozen
breakfasts? Not me. It is not so difficult to explain to a
three-year-old child what absent without leave means,

but absent from *what*, I doubt if I can explain that.
You become human when you go absent without leave
from your unit: I found this out, and offer it as candid
advice to later generations. (But watch out when they
start shooting! There are some idiots who aim to hit!)
For my granddaughter I just portray her as a genre
painter might: a pretty young woman leaning over the
sill of her attic window, watering her geraniums with a
yellow watering-can. Visible in the background are
Dostoevsky's "Idiot" next to Christian Morgenstern,
Grimms' Fairy Tales, and "Michael Kohlhaas" in the
kitchen closet between two china jars marked RICE
and SUGAR, in front of the closet a buggy containing
a babbling infant for whom someone (me! I beat my
breast in remorse) has made a rattle out of some old
uniform buckles and string. With the snooper's tele-
scope, one would be able to see on the buckles a spade
flanked by wheat ears. (Was that my mother? Yes.)
Whenever I choose the Holzmarkt and the Bayen-
Strasse for our walk, instead of the Leystapel and the
Frankenwerft, and consent to go along the boulevard
beside the Ubier Ring, a child's persistence drags me
relentlessly to the street whose name I once revealed,
whose location I once betrayed. (Where was the house?
Over there. Which was your room? Just about there.
How come my mother wasn't hit by the bomb? She was
at Grandmother's. You mean Great-Grandmother?

Yes.) I solemnly make her a promise I intend to keep: to read to her from "The Idiot," from "Michael Kohlhaas" and Christian Morgenstern; I have already read to her from Grimms' Fairy Tales. Our walks in the direction of the Bayen-Strasse usually end up at Great-Grandmother's. Coffee is drunk (not by me), cake is eaten (Rodons, elsewhere known as Gugelhupf, not by me), cigarettes are smoked (not by me), rosaries are said (not by me). While all this is going on, I clasp my hands behind my back, walk to the window, look across to the Severin Gate. Whenever airplanes appear over the city or—as the newspapers so charmingly put it— skim over it, I suddenly find myself in the grip of that almost epileptic twitching that is at the bottom of all the dispute over my health, and by this time, if not before, everyone must have realized what astute readers have perceived long ago: that I am a neurotic. These attacks often go on for a long time, on the way home I begin to drag my legs, jerk my arms. Recently a mother explained to her five-year-old son in a loud clear voice, pointing at me as she did so: "See that man? That's a typical case of Parkinson's disease"—which I am not. Sometimes the sight of steam-shovels sets me off jerking like that, and whispering to myself "Work makes us free," and this recently caused a young man behind me to say: "There's another one of those." Since —as a result of my head wound—I also stammer, and

the only words that flow smoothly from my lips are
those I sing, and what is more suitable for singing than
the lines "German women, German honor, German wine
and German song"? I have to hear "There's another
one of those" quite frequently. I am used to it. The
fact that my clean hands usually have dirty nails, that
I have never applied for a disabled veteran's pension,
which means I have no document to prove the origin of
my palpable impairments, gives rise to additional
"There's another one of those." I have no intention
whatever of making this concession to sound common
sense.

The only advice I accept is my mother-in-law's.
"You need a shave. Pay more attention to your business. Don't get annoyed over that fellow Berthen your
daughter was silly enough to marry. Doesn't anyone
sew your buttons on for you? Come here!"

It's true: I am not very good at sewing, and I shall
be glad to supply the coloring book with a dozen torn-
off buttons, both round and oblong, for each year of my
life from twenty-one to forty-eight. The reader may
transform and color the round buttons any way he
likes, and the oblong ones too. If he feels so inclined, he
may turn the round ones into daisies or asters, he can
also make them into coins or clocks, into full moons,
into pepper pots or wall plugs seen from above, any
round object is a legitimate button-variation for his

imagination. He can turn them into party badges, or St. Christopher medals. The oblong ones, the kind which are always sewn much too loosely onto duffel coats and related garments, can easily be turned into half-moons, croissants or commas, Christmas decorations or sickles. For each year up to 1949 I will generously fork out a dozen round and oblong buttons, and for each year after 1949 half a dozen, and I will also throw in a few worn-out zippers, excellent for turning into tangled undergrowth or barbed wire. Then the tiny shirt buttons—round ones only, I am afraid—we will just take a few handfuls of these and sprinkle them like sugar on a doughnut. Sock holes, shirt holes, even the great big ones, there are plenty of those, especially suitable for snoopers too, for, as the merest child knows (I repeat it here for the benefit of grown-ups with their short memories), there is nothing so archaeologically pregnant as a hole. A widower like me, who has always steadfastly refused to sew anything, just as he had steadfastly refused to clean his shoes, has holes to offer in abundance. Not long ago, one of the few shoeshine men to be found around here told me reproachfully: "I see you don't know how to look after your shoes." I am sure he used to be a sergeant-major, and Germans are born pedagogues. My mother-in-law is not a pedagogue, she just tugs gently at my clothes, picks fluff off my coat, straightens my shoulders by "arranging" the padding in my jacket and coat, she bends down (not to undo but) to tighten my shoelaces and tuck them in. She places my hat on my head at the angle she considers smart (meaning, the angle that used to be smart in the twenties), bursts into tears without warning, puts her arms around me, kisses me on both cheeks, and maintains I have always been more of a son to her than all her sons, except of course for Angel, "who was much more than a son." Her son Johannes she always refers to simply as a "sourpuss," her daughters-in-law as "nothing but nuisances" and her husband as a "renegade proletarian" who, now that he has even acquired a poodle (yellow collar, yellow leash) has ceased to exist for her. "If we were divorced, we couldn't be more divorced." And when she adds: "You're still absent without leave," I know what she means.

Now and again I invite her out to lunch, followed by a taxi ride through Cologne to give her a good look at how a destroyed city can destroy. I get a receipt for the dinner (she has a healthy appetite and appreciates "something special") and the taxi ride, and write on the receipt "discussion among business associates." My manager, who is as upright as he is accurate, suffers a slight bilious attack every time, first because it should be *with* instead of *among*, and then "because it is unethical." Recently when we were in a taxi my mother-in-law gave me a "penetrating" look with her dark eyes and said: "You know what you really could do, what you could take up?" "No," I said nervously. "You could go back to university," she said. And with that she managed to make me laugh for the first time in eighteen years, in a way which I can only describe as hearty. The last time I laughed that heartily was when an American lieutenant called me a "fuckin' German Nazi." Probably both are (were) right: my mother-in-law and the American lieutenant. At the time I sang in an undertone the words I now so often sing to myself almost compulsively, especially when I am sitting on the terrace of the Café Reichard: "German women, German honor, German wine and German song. . . ."

Sometimes we sit together on the café terrace, and, without expecting or making any comments, much less offering consolation, I let her cry quietly to herself, for her children who have died, and reflect on the fact that not one of her dead children has found a resting place in a churchyard. No grave to put flowers on, no dream or vision of that gentle, flowery peace which makes churchyards so appealing to romantics (like me), so full of healing to neurotics (like me), where under trees and shrubs, with widows weeding near by (strangely enough one hardly ever sees widowers weeding), they can meditate on the transitoriness of man's mortal self.

"Just opposite the cathedral," on the terrace of the Café Reichard, I have every reason to wish I was standing in the market square of Ballaghaderreen and could wait there for the next circus, due to arrive in about eight months.

When my granddaughter asks why her great-grandmother is crying, she has more in common with the waiters and their customers, who are embarrassed by an "oddly dressed, weeping old woman," than with us, and by asking such a question she puts us in the Neanderthal category. My daughter and son-in-law "flatly refuse" to go out with us. My daughter is sufficiently respectful not to analyze the reasons for this refusal, but my son-in-law describes us as being "something between half-witted and antisocial." My granddaughter still possesses the innocence that renders us fit company in her eyes. If I were to answer her question and tell her that here, six or eight feet away from us, one of her great-uncles had been executed, she would believe me less than her two great-grandfathers, who are so expert at dating their archaeological finds. And if I were to tell her that there are people who weep at gravesides, at places of execution, especially when one of those who were executed was her son, the child would probably already have learned that such sentiments derive merely from complexes or feelings of hostility. Even mention of the Blessed Virgin, who is said to have wept beside the Cross, would not preserve my mother-in-law from listening to such phrases, or my brother-in-law's execution from being vaguely seen by her in terms of a movie. Not because but although she is being brought up a Catholic, the child is past saving. She will wear her religion like a rare perfume that in a few years will have become a connoisseur's item.

While my mother-in-law is crying quietly, drying her tears with a handkerchief which is much too large, and my granddaughter is eating ice cream, I am busy inventing a genuinely Brazilian-sounding name for our bill which I intend to present to my conscientious manager for a tax voucher. I hesitate between Oliveira and Espinhaço, whom I hereby declare to be coffee planters or wholesalers and with whom I shall swear at any time to have had business discussions. I shall raise my right hand and swear to the authenticity of Oliveira or Espinhaço. I shall probably also add a Margarita or a Juanita, for whom I shall likewise swear to have ordered flowers sent to their hotel.

Is it necessary, since I have already confessed to being a tea drinker, to enlarge on what the coffee business means to me? Nothing, of course. I do not feel the slightest moral tie with this branch of business. I sign anything my manager puts before me without even looking at it. Now and again I am forced to participate in meetings with planters, wholesalers, or bankers, and needless to say I have hanging in my wardrobe for such purposes what is known as a "business suit."

My stammering and nervous twitching seem not only attractive but positively elegant. They lend me a certain air of decadence, enhanced by the fact that I ostentatiously drink tea. As soon as the conversation shows the faintest sign of becoming personal, I cut it off with a brief gesture and an expression meriting the epithet disgusted. I have never been one for familiarity, and "the human touch" has always reminded me too much of the inhuman touch. My son-in-law, who is present at these meetings and naturally admires my style in one way but in another way (understandably enough) detests it, looks at me as if I were an excavated statue which suddenly begins to move.

I am soon going to move in altogether with my mother-in-law, and probably follow her inspired advice to "go back to university." But I must wait till the business has been transferred to my son-in-law *de jure* and *de facto*. He has warned me himself, he has urged me, to read each paragraph in our contract very carefully "and not to rely on humanitarian feelings which in business life simply don't exist." This warning is almost humane, at any rate it is conscientious, and since I do not trust conscientious people who have no style, I shall read the contract carefully. Old Mr. Bechtold gave up his room long ago, but there are still some leather samples lying around in it, and his cobbler's stool is still there (he carted it around with him each of the five times they moved house), although from the day I threw dice with his sons over who should join the S.A. he never repaired another shoe. The walls will have to be repapered, my furniture will have to be moved in there. Anna Bechtold has set up a program for our life together: "Studying while absent without leave." I have promised her that finally, after more than twenty years, I will find out what was meant by the "Rhenish florin" Hildegard was so excited about the evening before she was killed, when she brought little Hildegard over to her grandmother's. We shall, of course, be "at home to relatives," we have no intention, if only because of the necessity of obtaining food supplies, of walling up our front door. Johannes, the "sourpuss," will come, her "tiresome daughters-in-law," her grandchildren and great-grandchildren. My son-in-law will come now and again and with a crafty smile give me to understand that he has managed to cheat me, and his conscience will be perfectly clear for, after all, he did warn me. I shall even put up with my mother-in-law's romantic notions of "student's digs." As she is experienced in dealing with "furnished gentlemen," I accept her ideas, since I have none myself, of "smartness" (as it was in the twenties) which so far she has only been able to put into practice with my hats. She has even agreed to make a study of the preparation of tea.

Have I already mentioned that, although she is not

illiterate, she can hardly write at all, and that she has chosen me as the one to whom she wishes to dictate her memoirs: with the blackest possible ink on the whitest possible paper? If I have not mentioned it before, I do so now.

IX

My son-in-law has requested that, since I am giving away family secrets, I insert "a little more publicity, even if it is negative," for him and his wife. As far as my daughter is concerned, I find myself in an awkward situation: by the end of the war, when she was four years old, she had been through one thousand air raids (my mother-in-law refused to leave Cologne, "you see, two of my children died here")—and I have no right to object to a certain hunger for life on the part of my daughter which manifests itself outwardly in an anxious materialism. Even her very best qualities—she doesn't talk much, and she is generous—are rooted in anxiety. She has little patience with me (owing to certain injuries I am slow—dressing and undressing, eating, and my occasional attacks fill her with ill-concealed disgust), but I am only too willing to forgive her ten embarrassments for every air raid, and in this way she has an inexhaustible credit. The disappointing fact that she resembles me rather than Hildegard (which gives her more grounds for annoyance than it does me) increases her credit. Her piety is also anxiety-ridden: precise, law-abiding, and because of her mixed marriage she is at present wrapped up in a church council euphoria which will gradually abate like the effect of a drug. The smile we exchange whenever we meet is merely another way of shrugging our shoulders. She is completely under the influence of my father and father-in-law, and already assiduously collecting "little antique pieces" with which to furnish my rooms when I leave. With the eye of an interior decorator she is already moving my furniture out and her own in, measuring distances, gauging effects, matching colors, and I would be neither surprised nor hurt if I came home unexpectedly one day and found her with a tape measure in her hand. That is unlikely; my lopsided walk, coupled with a leg injury, make me both slow and noisy when I climb the stairs and give ample notice of my arrival. Apropos of my stair-climbing technique, I have more than once heard the word "snail." But no one has given me the snail's blessing yet, and there has been no talk of making a man of me or carrying ordure. Sometimes I am also called an "idealist" because I have not claimed a disabled veteran's pension. I am of the modest opinion that my motives are of a more realistic nature and have to do with my anancastia. Even the study of masculine absurdity—equally useful both quantitatively and qualitatively speaking—which I could not avoid making during the war, is something I regard as an unpleasant enrichment. I am still capable of pity for this masculine absurdity, but not of respect. I shall not become resigned, I shall study, which is perhaps—and not only in my case—a form of resignation.

Anyone looking for me will find me at the spot where, without having to crane one's neck, it is possible to look across to the Severin Gate.

POSTSCRIPTA

A Jew by a bellow, a German by a kiss,
a Christian by baptism

1. *Detailed Confession.* I did not succeed in describing the expression on the faces of the two Bechtolds when I had beaten them at the dice game: respect, amazement, mingled with hysterical mortification and resignation, and when I suggested that as a son-in-law I take over the function of a son and join the S.A., they

howled with rage: what they wanted was to see Angel sullied with the stain of being a Stormtrooper.

That all I offer of my mother is one or two dots has its reasons: she was too fragile, she might fall apart, or the result might be too unsatisfactory, so I would rather each person stick a cliché, a decal, or something of the sort, into the coloring book: middle-class lady circa 1938, mid-forties, delicate but not languishing. Nauseated yes, but not for sociological reasons.

I have already acknowledged to being a romantic, a neurotic, an idyllist; I reiterate it here for the benefit of grown-ups.

I have known for twenty years what was meant by the "Rhenish florin" Hildegard was so excited about. The compulsory mutual fellowship camp where I received the snail's blessing, became a Jew by being bellowed at, was banished to the ordure section to become a man, and met Angel, was situated in the heart of the forest in which many of the Grimm fairy tales originate. I received most of the commands, punishments and blessings meted out by the officers there in the dialect which must have been spoken by the peasant woman who told the Grimm brothers the fairy tales. Is it any wonder that I gave Hildegard "Michael Kohlhaas" and Grimms' Fairy Tales for a wedding present ("The Idiot" and Christian Morgenstern were part of her dowry), that she read them a great deal and that the story called "How the Children Played at Butchering" made the deepest impression on her, that is to say, seemed to her the most topical. She must have known it by heart, the story about the innocent child reaching for the apple instead of the coin, for she used to repeat over and over again the phrase my mother-in-law could never understand: "They're taking the Rhenish florin —the Rhenish florin!" So I know the background, a rather involved one—but I can't bring myself to explain it to my mother-in-law. Even in my own mind, a lot of it is *supposition*. But I have no doubt whatever as to the topical nature of the "Rhenish florin." Who would choose the apple, when the merest child knows that for a florin you could probably buy a hundred apples? Everyone has been playing at Butchering, and they were not children, and innocence is not a coin. By adding that since my wife's death I have lived chastely, I have at least put the finishing touch to the embarrassment, and the reader may laugh long and lustily. And when I add that *my* favorite fairy tale is the one about the Singing Bone, the laughter will grow louder still.

2. *Moral.* I urge everyone to go absent without leave. Defection and desertion I would advise in favor of rather than against, for as I said: there are idiots who aim to hit, and everyone ought to realize the risk they

are running. Firearms are instruments completely lacking in humor. I recall Angel, and Anton Bechtold.

To go absent without leave from irregular troops is
particularly dangerous because this—most thinking
people do not think far enough—gives rise automati-
cally, as it were, to the suspicion that the would-be ab-
sentee wishes to join the regular troops; so, watch out.

3. *Interpretation*

(a) The three (white) officers' handkerchiefs given
to the nuns are transmuted lilies, like the ones found in
front of the altars of St. Joseph, the Blessed Virgin,
and virgin saints in general. They stand in direct rela-
tionship to the whitest *possible* paper, to the obsessional hand-washing, and the aversion to inspections
and cleaning one's own shoes, to the manifest passion
for cleanliness. How otherwise would anyone perpetrate
a theft of army property for the sake of a few baths—
for, although the coal came from the Lorraine, it belonged *by rights* to the German Army—and to carry
on such complicated negotiations with nuns of all people denotes a complete and utter Platonism.

On the other hand, the frequent mention of ordure,
dirty nails, and the well-nigh ecstatic portrayal of his
own weaknesses: attacks of near-epilepsy, severe difficulty in walking, the morbid dislike of airplane noises
which precipitate such attacks—all this permits the

conclusion that the narrator is right to call himself a neurotic, and is right to describe himself as romantic and resigned. The élitist elements—even when the subject is an élite among ordure carriers—are also unmistakable. And has the dislike for the "Rhenish florin" anything to do with the (totally incomprehensible) refusal to apply for and accept whatever is "due" to him for his war injuries and disabilities?

(b) The mention of Hänsel and Gretel is traceable to a simple set of facts: in the forest the narrator absented himself several times from the group of workers, wandered around with a piece of bread in his pocket— and it was on these occasions that he missed "Gretel's comforting hand." The fact that the author mentions "The Singing Bone" as a third and favorite fairy tale denotes a connection with the "Rhenish florin."

(c) The attempt to equate study with resignation, or at least to imply their identity, is attributable to an early deep-seated dislike of botanical specimen boxes.

(d) Engel(bert) is not meant to symbolize an angel, although that is what he was called and what he is described as looking like.

(e) The narrator is concealing something. What?

Enter and Exit

a novella in two parts

when the war broke out

I was leaning out of the window, my arms resting on the sill, I had rolled up my shirtsleeves and was looking beyond the main gate and guardroom across to the divisional headquarters telephone exchange, waiting for my friend Leo to give me the prearranged signal: come to the window, take off his cap, and put it on again. Whenever I got the chance I would lean out of the window, my arms on the sill; whenever I got the chance I would call a girl in Cologne and my mother—at army expense—and when Leo came to the window, took off his cap, and put it on again, I would run down to the barrack square and wait in the public callbox till the phone rang.

The other telephone operators sat there bareheaded, in their undershirts, and when they leaned forward to plug in or unplug, or to push up a flap, their identity disks would dangle out of their undershirts and fall

back again when they straightened up. Leo was the
only one wearing a cap, just so he could take it off to
give me the signal. He had a heavy, pink face, very fair
hair, and came from Oldenburg. The first expression
you noticed on his face was guileless; the second was:
incredibly guileless, and no one paid enough attention
to Leo to notice more than those two expressions; he
looked as uninteresting as the boys whose faces appear
on advertisements for cheese.

It was hot, afternoon; the alert that had been going
on for days had become stale, transforming all time as
it passed into stillborn Sunday hours. The barrack
square lay there blind and empty, and I was glad I
could at least keep my head out of the camaraderie of
my roommates. Over there the operators were plugging
and unplugging, pushing up flaps, wiping off sweat,
and Leo was sitting there among them, his cap on his
thick fair hair.

All of a sudden I noticed the rhythm of plugging
and unplugging had altered; arm movements were no
longer routine, mechanical, they became hesitant, and
Leo threw his arms up over his head three times: a signal we had not arranged but from which I could tell
that something out of the ordinary had happened; then
I saw an operator take his steel helmet from the switchboard and put it on; he looked ridiculous, sitting there
sweating in his undershirt, his identity disk dangling,
his steel helmet on his head—but I couldn't laugh at

him; I realized that putting on a steel helmet meant
something like "ready for action," and I was scared.

The ones who had been dozing on their beds behind
me in the room got up, lit cigarettes, and formed the
two customary groups: three probationary teachers,
who were still hoping to be discharged as being "essential to the nation's educational system," resumed their
discussion of Ernst Jünger; the other two, an orderly
and an office clerk, began discussing the female form;
they didn't tell dirty stories, they didn't laugh, they
discussed it just as two exceptionally boring geography
teachers might have discussed the conceivably interesting topography of the Ruhr valley. Neither subject
interested me. Psychologists, those interested in psychology, and those about to complete an adult educa-
tion course in psychology, may be interested to learn
that my desire to call the girl in Cologne became more
urgent than in previous weeks; I went to my locker,
took out my cap, put it on, and leaned out of the window, my arms on the sill, wearing my cap: the signal
for Leo that I had to speak to him at once. To show he
understood, he waved to me, and I put on my tunic,
went out of the room, down the stairs, and stood at the
entrance to headquarters, waiting for Leo.

It was hotter than ever, quieter than ever, the barrack squares were even emptier, and nothing has ever

approximated my idea of hell as closely as hot, silent,
empty barrack squares. Leo came very quickly; he was
also wearing his steel helmet now, and was displaying
one of his other five expressions which I knew: dangerous for everything he didn't like; this was the face he
sat at the switchboard with when he was on evening or
night duty, listened in on secret official calls, told me
what they were about, suddenly jerked out plugs, cut
off secret official calls so as to put through an urgent
secret call to Cologne, for me to talk to the girl; then it
would be my turn to work the switchboard, and Leo
would first call his girl in Oldenburg, then his father;
meanwhile Leo would cut thick slices from the ham his
mother had sent him, cut these into cubes, and we would
eat cubes of ham. When things were slack, Leo would
teach me the art of recognizing the caller's rank from
the way the flaps fell; at first I thought it was enough
to be able to tell the rank simply by the force with
which the flap fell: corporal, sergeant, etc., but Leo
could tell exactly whether it was an officious corporal
or a tired colonel demanding a line; from the way the
flap fell he could even distinguish between angry captains and annoyed lieutenants—nuances which are
very hard to tell apart, and as the evening went on his
other expressions made their appearance: fixed hatred;
primordial malice; with these faces he would suddenly
become pedantic, articulate his "Are you still talk-

ing?", his "Yessirs," with great care, and with un-
nerving rapidity switch plugs so as to turn an official
call about boots into one about boots and ammunition,
and the other call about ammunition into one about
ammunition and boots, or the private conversation of a
sergeant-major with his wife might be suddenly inter-
rupted by a lieutenant's voice saying: "I insist the
man be punished, I absolutely insist." With lightning
speed Leo would then switch the plugs over so that the
boot partners were talking about boots again and the
others about ammunition, and the sergeant-major's
wife could resume discussion of her stomach trouble
with her husband. When the ham was all gone, Leo's
relief had arrived, and we were walking across the silent barrack square to our room, Leo's face would
wear its final expression: foolish, innocent in a way
that had nothing to do with childlike innocence.

Any other time I would have laughed at Leo, standing there wearing his steel helmet, that symbol of in-
flated importance. He looked past me, across the first,
the second barrack square, to the stables; his expressions alternated from three to five, from five to four,
and with his final expression he said: "It's war, war,
war—they finally made it." I said nothing, and he said:
"I guess you want to talk to her?" "Yes," I said.

"I've already talked to mine," he said. "She's not

pregnant, I don't know whether to be glad or not. What d'you think?" "You can be glad," I said, "I don't think it's a good idea to have kids in wartime."

"General mobilization," he said, "state of alert, this place is soon going to be swarming—and it'll be a long while before you and I can go off on our bikes again." (When we were off duty we used to ride our bikes out into the country, onto the moors, the farmers' wives used to fix us fried eggs and thick slices of bread and butter.) "The first joke of the war has already happened," said Leo: "In view of my special skills and services in connection with the telephone system, I have been made a corporal—now go over to the public callbox, and if it doesn't ring in three minutes I'll demote myself for incompetence."

In the callbox I leaned against the "Münster Area" phone book, lit a cigarette, and looked out through a gap in the frosted glass across the barrack square; the only person I could see was a sergeant-major's wife, in Block 4 I think; she was watering her geraniums from a yellow jug; I waited, looked at my wristwatch: one minute, two, and I was startled when it actually rang, and even more startled when I immediately heard the voice of the girl in Cologne: "Maybach's Furniture Company," and I said: "Marie, it's war, it's war"— and she said: "No." I said: "Yes it is," then there was

silence for half a minute, and she said: "Shall I come?",
and before I could say spontaneously, instinctively,
"Yes, please do," the voice of what was probably a
fairly senior officer shouted: "We need ammunition,
and we need it urgently." The girl said: "Are you still
there?" The officer yelled: "God damn it!" Meanwhile I
had had time to wonder about what it was in the girl's
voice that had sounded unfamiliar, ominous almost: her
voice had sounded like marriage, and I suddenly knew I
didn't feel like marrying her. I said: "We're probably
pulling out tonight." The officer yelled: "God damn it,
God damn it!" (evidently he couldn't think of anything better to say), the girl said: "I could catch the
four o'clock train and be there just before seven," and I
said, more quickly than was polite: "It's too late,
Marie, too late"—then all I heard was the officer, who
seemed to be on the verge of apoplexy. He screamed:
"Well, do we get the ammunition or don't we?" And I
said in a steely voice (I had learned that from Leo):
"No, no, you don't get any ammunition, even if it
chokes you." Then I hung up.

It was still daylight when we loaded boots from railway cars onto trucks, but by the time we were loading
boots from trucks onto railway cars it was dark, and it
was still dark when we loaded boots from railway cars
onto trucks again, then it was daylight again, and we

loaded bales of hay from trucks onto railway cars, and it was still daylight, and we were still loading bales of hay from trucks onto railway cars; but then it was dark again, and for exactly twice as long as we had loaded bales of hay from trucks onto railway cars, we loaded bales of hay from railway cars onto trucks. At one point a field kitchen arrived, in full combat rig, we were given large helpings of goulash and small helpings of potatoes, and we were given real coffee and cigarettes which we didn't have to pay for; that must have been at night, for I remember hearing a voice say: real coffee and cigarettes for free, the surest sign of war; I don't remember the face belonging to this voice. It was daylight again when we marched back to barracks, and as we turned into the street leading past the barracks we met the first battalion going off. It was headed by a marching band playing "Must I then, must I then," followed by the first company, then their armored vehicles, then the second, third and finally the fourth with the heavy machine guns. On not one face, not one single face, did I see the least sign of enthusiasm; of course there were some people standing on the sidewalks, some girls too, but not once did I see anybody stick a bunch of flowers onto a soldier's rifle; there was not even the merest trace of a sign of enthusiasm in the air.

Leo's bed was untouched; I opened his locker (a de-

gree of familiarity with Leo which the probationary
teachers, shaking their heads, called "going too far");
everything was in its place: the photo of the girl in
Oldenburg, she was standing, leaning against her bi-
cycle, in front of a birch tree; photos of Leo's parents;
their farmhouse. Next to the ham there was a message:
"Transferred to area headquarters. In touch with you
soon, take all the ham, I've taken what I need. Leo." I
didn't take any of the ham, and closed the locker; I was
not hungry, and the rations for two days had been
stacked up on the table: bread, cans of liver sausage,
butter, cheese, jam and cigarettes. One of the probationary teachers, the one I liked least, announced that
he had been promoted to Pfc and appointed room senior
for the period of Leo's absence; he began to distribute
the rations; it took a very long time; the only thing I
was interested in was the cigarettes, and these he left to
the last because he was a nonsmoker. When I finally got
the cigarettes I tore open the pack, lay down on the bed
in my clothes and smoked; I watched the others eating.
They spread liver sausage an inch thick on the bread
and discussed the "excellent quality of the butter," then
they drew the black-out blinds and lay down on their
beds; it was very hot, but I didn't feel like undressing;
the sun shone into the room through a few cracks, and
in one of these strips of light sat the newly promoted
Pfc sewing on his Pfc's chevron. It isn't so easy to sew

on a Pfc's chevron: it has to be placed at a certain prescribed distance from the seam of the sleeve; moreover, the two open sides of the chevron must be absolutely straight; the probationary teacher had to take off the chevron several times, he sat there for at least two hours, unpicking it, sewing it back on, and he did not appear to be running out of patience; outside the band came marching by every forty minutes, and I heard the "Must I then, must I then," from Block 7, Block 2, from Block 9, then from over by the stables— it would come closer, get very loud, then softer again; it took almost exactly three "Must I thens" for the Pfc to sew on his chevron, and it still wasn't quite straight; by that time I had smoked the last of my cigarettes and fell asleep.

That afternoon we didn't have to load either boots from trucks onto railway cars or bales of hay from railway cars onto trucks; we had to help the quartermaster-sergeant; he considered himself a genius at organization; he had requisitioned as many assistants as there were items of clothing and equipment on his list, except that for the groundsheets he needed two; he also required a clerk. The two men with the groundsheets went ahead and laid them out, flicking the corners nice and straight, neatly on the cement floor of the stable; as soon as the groundsheets had been spread out, the first

man started off by laying two neckties on each groundsheet; the second man, two handkerchiefs; I came next
with the mess kits, and while all the articles in which, as
the sergeant said, size was not a factor, were being distributed, he was preparing, with the aid of the more
intelligent members of the detachment, the objects in
which size was a factor: tunics, boots, trousers, and so
on; he had a whole pile of paybooks lying there, he
selected the tunics, trousers and boots according to
measurements and weight, and he insisted everything
would fit, "unless the bastards have got too fat as civilians"; it all had to be done at great speed, in one continuous operation, and it was done at great speed, in
one continuous operation, and when everything had
been spread out the reservists came in, were conducted
to their groundsheets, tied the ends together, hoisted
their bundles onto their backs, and went to their rooms
to put on their uniforms. Only occasionally did something have to be exchanged, and then it was always
because someone had got too fat as a civilian. It was
also only occasionally that something was missing: a
shoe-cleaning brush or a spoon or fork, and it always
turned out that someone else had two shoe-cleaning
brushes or two spoons or forks, a fact which confirmed
the sergeant's theory that we did not work mechanically
enough, that we were "still using our brains too much."
I didn't use my brain at all, with the result that no one

was short a mess kit. While the first man of each company being equipped was hoisting his bundle onto his shoulder, the first of our own lot had to start spreading out the next groundsheet; everything went smoothly; meanwhile the newly promoted Pfc sat at the table and wrote everything down in the paybooks; most of the time he had only to enter a one in the paybook, except with the neckties, socks, handkerchiefs, undershirts and underpants, where he had to write a two.

In spite of everything, though, there were occasionally some dead minutes, as the quartermaster-sergeant called them, and we were allowed to use these to fortify ourselves; we would sit on the bunks in the grooms' quarters and eat bread and liver sausage, sometimes bread and cheese or bread and jam, and when the sergeant had a few dead minutes himself he would come over and give us a lecture about the difference between rank and appointment; he found it tremendously interesting that he himself was a quartermaster-sergeant—"that's my appointment"—and yet had the rank of a corporal, "that's my rank," in this way, so he said, there was no reason, for example, why a Pfc should not act as a quartermaster-sergeant, indeed even an ordinary private might; he found the theme endlessly fascinating and kept on concocting new examples, some of which betokened a well-nigh treasonable imagination: "It can actually happen, for instance," he said, "that a Pfc is put in command of a company, of a battalion even."

For ten hours I laid mess kits on groundsheets, slept for six hours, and again for ten hours laid mess kits on groundsheets; then I slept another six hours and had still heard nothing from Leo. When the third ten hours of laying out mess kits began, the Pfc started entering a two wherever there should have been a one, and a one wherever there should have been a two. He was relieved of his post, and now had to lay out neckties, and the second probationary teacher was appointed clerk. I stayed with the mess kits during the third ten hours too, the sergeant said he thought I had done surprisingly well.

During the dead minutes, while we were sitting on the bunks eating bread and cheese, bread and jam, bread and liver sausage, strange rumors were beginning to be peddled around. A story was being told about a rather well-known retired general who received orders by phone to go to a small island in the North Sea where he was to assume a top-secret, extremely important command; the general had taken his uniform out of the closet, kissed his wife, children and grandchildren goodbye, given his favorite horse a farewell pat, and taken the train to some station on the North Sea and from there hired a motorboat to the island in question; he had been foolish enough to send back the motorboat before ascertaining the nature of his command; he was cut off by the rising tide and—so the story went—had forced the farmer on the island at pistol point to risk his life and row him back to the mainland. By afternoon there was already a variation to the tale: some sort of a struggle had taken place in the boat between the general and the farmer, they had both been swept overboard and drowned. What I couldn't stand was that this story—and a number of others—was considered criminal all right, but funny as well, while to me they seemed neither one nor the other; I couldn't accept the grim accusation of sabotage, which was being used like some kind of moral tuning-fork, nor could I join in the laughter or grin with the others. The war seemed to deprive what was funny of its funny side.

At any other time the "Must I thens" which ran through my dreams, my sleep, and my few waking moments, the countless men who got off the streetcars and came hurrying into the barracks with their cardboard boxes and went out again an hour later with "Must I then"; even the speeches which we sometimes listened to with half an ear, speeches in which the words united effort were always occurring—all this I would have found funny, but everything which would have been funny before was not funny any more, and I could no longer laugh or smile at all the things which would have seemed laughable; not even the sergeant, and not even the Pfc, whose chevron was still not quite straight and who sometimes laid out three neckties on the groundsheet instead of two.

It was still hot, still August, and the fact that three times sixteen hours are only forty-eight, two days and two nights, was something I didn't realize until I woke up about eleven on Sunday and for the first time since Leo had been transferred was able to lean out of the window, my arms on the sill; the probationary teachers, wearing their walking-out dress, were ready for church and looked at me in a challenging kind of way, but all I said was: "Go ahead, I'll follow you," and it was obvious that they were glad to be able to go without me for once. Whenever we had gone to church they had looked at me as if they would like to excommunicate me, because something or other about me or my uniform was not quite up to scratch in their eyes: the way my boots were cleaned, the way I had tied my tie, my belt or my hair-cut; they were indignant not as fellow-soldiers (which, objectively speaking, I agree would have been justified), but as Catholics; they would rather I had not made it so unmistakably clear that we were actually going to one and the same church; it embarrassed them, but there wasn't a thing they could do about it, because my paybook is marked: R.C.

This Sunday there was no mistaking how glad they were to be able to go without me, I had only to watch them marching off to town, past the barracks, clean, upright, and brisk. Sometimes, when I felt bouts of pity for them, I was glad for their sakes that Leo was a Protestant: I think they simply couldn't have borne it if Leo had been a Catholic too.

The office clerk and the orderly were still asleep; we didn't have to be at the stable again till three that afternoon. I stood leaning out of the window for a while, till it was time to go, so as to get to church just in time to miss the sermon. Then, while I was dressing, I opened Leo's locker again: to my surprise it was empty, except for a piece of paper and a big chunk of ham; Leo had locked the cupboard again to be sure I would find the message and the ham. On the paper was written: "This is it—I'm being sent to Poland—did you get my message?" I put the paper in my pocket, turned the key in the locker, and finished dressing; I was in a daze as I walked into town and entered the church, and even the glances of the three probationary teachers, who turned round to look at me and then back to the altar again, shaking their heads, failed to rouse me completely. Probably they wanted to make sure quickly whether I hadn't come in *after* the Elevation of the Host so they could apply for my excommunication; but I really had arrived *before* the Elevation, there was nothing they could do, besides I wanted to remain a Catholic. I thought of Leo and was scared, I thought too of the girl in Cologne and had a twinge of conscience, but I was sure her voice had sounded like marriage. To annoy my roommates, I undid my collar while I was still in church.

After Mass I stood outside leaning against the church wall in a shady corner between the vestry and the door, took off my cap, lit a cigarette, and watched the faithful as they left the church and walked past me. I wondered how I could get hold of a girl with whom I could go for a walk, have a cup of coffee, and maybe go to a movie; I still had three hours before I had to lay out mess kits on groundsheets again. It would be nice if the girl were not too silly and reasonably pretty. I also thought about dinner at the barracks, which I was missing now, and that perhaps I ought to have told the office clerk he could have my chop and dessert.

I smoked two cigarettes while I stood there, watching the faithful standing about in twos and threes, then separating again, and just as I was lighting the third cigarette from the second a shadow fell across me from one side, and when I looked to the right I saw that the person casting the shadow was even blacker than the shadow itself: it was the chaplain who had read Mass. He looked very kind, not old, thirty perhaps, fair and just a shade too well-fed. First he looked at my open collar, then at my boots, then at my bare head, and finally at my cap, which I had put next to me on a ledge where it had slipped off onto the paving; last of all he looked at my cigarette, then into my face, and I had the feeling that he didn't like anything he saw there. "What's the matter?" he finally asked, "Are you in trouble?" And hardly had I nodded in reply to this question when he said: "Do you wish to confess?" Damn it, I thought, all they ever think of is confession, and only a certain part of that even. "No," I said, "I don't wish to confess." "Well then?" he said, "what's on your mind?" He might just as well have been asking about my stomach as my mind. He was obviously very impatient, looked at my cap, and I felt he was annoyed that I hadn't picked it up yet. I would have liked to turn his impatience into patience, but after all it wasn't I who had spoken to him, but he who had spoken to me, so I asked—to my annoyance, somewhat falteringly— whether he knew of some nice girl who would go for a walk with me, have a cup of coffee and maybe go to a movie in the evening; she didn't have to be a beauty queen, but she must be reasonably pretty, and if possible not from a good family, as these girls are usually so silly. I could give him the address of a chaplain in Cologne where he could make inquiries, call up if necessary, to satisfy himself I was from a good Catholic

home. I talked a lot, toward the end a bit more coher-
ently, and noticed how his face altered: at first it was
almost kind, it had almost looked benign, that was in
the early stage when he took me for a highly interesting, possibly even fascinating case of feeblemindedness
and found me psychologically quite amusing. The
transitions from kind to almost benign, from almost
benign to amused were hard to distinguish, but then
all of a sudden—the moment I mentioned the physical
attributes the girl was to have—he went purple with
rage. I was scared, for my mother had once told me it is
a sign of danger when overweight people suddenly go
purple in the face. Then he began to shout at me, and
shouting has always put me on edge. He shouted that I
looked a mess, with my "field tunic" undone, my boots
unpolished, my cap lying next to me "in the dirt, yes in
the dirt," and how undisciplined I was, smoking one
cigarette after another, and whether perhaps I couldn't
tell the difference between a Catholic priest and a pimp.
With my nerves strung up as they were I had stopped
being scared of him, I was just plain angry. I asked
him what my tie, my boots, my cap, had to do with him,
whether he thought maybe he had to do my corporal's
job, and: "Anyway," I said, "you fellows tell us all the
time to come to you with our troubles, and when someone really tells you his troubles you get mad." "You
fellows, eh?" he said, gasping with rage, "since when

are we on such familiar terms?" "We're not on any terms at all," I said. I picked up my cap, put it on without looking at it, and left, walking straight across the church square. He called after me to at least do up my tie, and I shouldn't be so stubborn; I very nearly turned round and shouted that *he* was the stubborn one, but then I remembered my mother telling me it was all right to be frank with a priest but you should try and avoid being impertinent—and so, without looking back, I went on into town. I left my tie dangling and thought about Catholics; there was a war on, but the first thing they looked at was your tie, then your boots. They said you should tell them your troubles, and when you did they got mad.

I walked slowly through town, on the lookout for a café where I wouldn't have to salute anyone; this stupid saluting spoiled all cafés for me; I looked at all the girls I passed, I turned round to look at them, at their legs even, but there wasn't one whose voice would not have sounded like marriage. I was desperate, I thought of Leo, of the girl in Cologne, I was on the point of sending her a telegram; I was almost prepared to risk getting married just to be alone with a girl. I stopped in front of the window of a photographer's studio, so I could think about Leo in peace. I was scared for him. I

saw my reflection in the shop window—my tie undone
and my black boots unpolished, I raised my hands to
button up my collar, but then it seemed too much trouble, and I dropped my hands again. The photographs
in the studio window were very depressing. They were
almost all of soldiers in walking-out dress; some had
even had their pictures taken wearing their steel helmets, and I was wondering whether the ones in steel
helmets were more depressing than the ones in peak
caps when a sergeant came out of the shop carrying a
framed photograph: the photo was fairly large, at least
twenty-four by thirty, the frame was painted silver,
and the picture showed the sergeant in walking-out
dress and steel helmet; he was quite young, not much
older than I was, twenty-one at most; he was just about
to walk past me, he hesitated, stopped, and I was wondering whether to raise my hand and salute him, when
he said: "Forget it—but if I were you I'd do up your
collar, and your tunic too, the next guy might be
tougher than I am." Then he laughed and went off, and
ever since then I have preferred (relatively, of course)
the ones who have their pictures taken in steel helmets
to the ones who have their pictures taken in peak caps.

Leo would have been just the person to stand with me
in front of the photo studio and look at the pictures;
there were also some bridal couples, first communicants,

and students wearing colored ribbons and fancy fobs over their stomachs, and I stood there wondering why they didn't wear ribbons in their hair; some of them wouldn't have looked bad in them at all. I needed company and had none.

Probably the chaplain thought I was suffering from lust, or that I was an anticlerical Nazi; but I was neither suffering from lust, nor was I anticlerical or a Nazi. I simply needed company, and not male company either, and that was so simple that it was terribly complicated; of course there were loose women in town as well as prostitutes (it was a Catholic town), but the loose women and the prostitutes were always offended if you weren't suffering from lust.

I stood for a long time in front of the photo studio; to this day I still always look at photo studios in strange cities; they are all much the same, and all equally depressing, although not everywhere do you find students with colored ribbons. It was nearly one o'clock when I finally left, on the lookout for a café where I didn't have to salute anyone, but in all the cafés they were sitting around in their uniforms, and I ended up by going to a movie anyway, to the first show at one-fifteen. All I remember was the newsreel: some very ignoble-looking Poles were maltreating some very noble-looking Germans; it was so empty in the movie

that I could risk smoking during the show; it was hot
that last Sunday in August 1939.

When I got back to barracks it was way past three;
for some reason the order to put down groundsheets at
three o'clock and spread out mess kits and neckties on
them had been countermanded; I came in just in time
to change, have some bread and liver sausage, lean out
of the window for a few minutes, listen to snatches of
the discussion about Ernst Jünger and the other one
about the female form; both discussions had become
more serious, more boring; the orderly and the office
clerk were now weaving Latin expressions into their re-
marks, and that made the whole thing even more re-
pulsive than it was in the first place.

At four we were called out, and I had imagined we
would be loading boots from trucks onto railways cars
again or from railway cars onto trucks, but this time we
loaded cases of soap powder, which were stacked up in
the gym, onto trucks, and from the trucks we unloaded
them at the parcel post office, where they were stacked
up again. The cases were not heavy, the addresses were
typewritten; we formed a chain, and so one case after
another passed through my hands; we did this the
whole of Sunday afternoon right through till late at
night, and there were scarcely any dead minutes when

we could have had a bite to eat; as soon as a truck was fully loaded, we drove to the main post office, formed a chain again, and unloaded the cases. Sometimes we overtook a Must-I-then column, or met one coming the other way; by this time they had three bands, and it was all going much faster. It was late, after midnight, when we had driven off with the last of the cases, and my hands remembered the number of mess kits and decided there was very little difference between cases of soap powder and mess kits.

I was very tired and wanted to throw myself on the bed fully dressed, but once again there was a great stack of bread and cans of liver sausage, jam and butter, on the table, and the others insisted it be distributed; all I wanted was the cigarettes, and I had to wait till everything had been divided up exactly, for of course the Pfc left the cigarettes to the last again; he took an abnormally long time about it, perhaps to teach me moderation and discipline and to convey his contempt for my craving; when I finally got the cigarettes, I lay down on the bed in my clothes and smoked and watched them spreading their bread with liver sausage, listened to them praising the excellent quality of the butter, and arguing mildly as to whether the jam was made of strawberries, apples and apricots, or of strawberries and apples only. They went on eating for a long time, and I couldn't fall asleep; then I heard footsteps coming along the passage and knew they were for me: I was afraid, and yet relieved, and the strange thing was that they all, the office clerk, the orderly and the three probationary teachers who were sitting round the table, stopped their chewing and looked at me as the footsteps drew closer; now the Pfc found it necessary to shout at me; he got up and yelled, calling me by my surname: "Damn it, take your boots off when you lie down."

There are certain things one refuses to believe, and I still don't believe it, although my ears remember quite well that all of a sudden he called me by my surname; I would have preferred it if we had used surnames all along, but coming so suddenly like that it sounded so funny that, for the first time since the war started, I had to laugh. Meanwhile the door had been flung open and the company clerk was standing by my bed; he was pretty excited, so much so that he didn't bawl me out, although he was a corporal, for lying on the bed with my boots and clothes on, smoking. He said: "You there, in twenty minutes in full marching order in Block 4, understand?" I said: "Yes" and got up. He added: "Report to the sergeant-major over there," and again I said yes and began to clear out my locker. I hadn't realized the company clerk was still in the room; I was just putting the picture of the girl in my trouser pocket when I heard him say: "I have some bad news, it's going to be tough on you but it should make you proud too; the first man from this regiment to be killed in action was your roommate, Corporal Leo Siemers."

I had turned round during the last half of this sentence, and they were all looking at me now, including the corporal; I had gone quite pale, and I didn't know whether to be furious or silent; then I said in a low voice: "But war hasn't been declared yet, he can't have been killed—and he wouldn't have been killed," and I shouted suddenly: "Leo wouldn't get killed, not him . . . you know he wouldn't." No one said anything, not even the corporal, and while I cleared out my locker and crammed all the stuff we were told to take with us into my pack, I heard him leave the room. I piled up all the things on the stool so I didn't have to turn around; I couldn't hear a sound from the others, I couldn't even hear them chewing. I packed all my stuff very quickly; the bread, liver sausage, cheese and butter I left in the locker and turned the key. When I had to turn around I saw they had managed to get into bed without a sound; I threw my locker key onto the office clerk's bed, saying: "Clear out everything that's still in there, it's all yours." I didn't care for him much, but I liked him best of the five; later on I was sorry I hadn't left without saying a word, but I was not yet twenty. I slammed the door, took my rifle from the rack outside, went down the stairs and saw from the

clock over the office door downstairs that it was nearly
three in the morning. It was quiet and still warm that
last Monday of August 1939. I threw Leo's locker key
somewhere onto the barrack square as I went across to
Block 4. They were all there, the band was already
moving into position at the head of the company, and
some officer who had given the united effort speech
was walking across the square, he took off his cap, wiped
the sweat from his forehead and put his cap on again.
He reminded me of a streetcar conductor who takes a
short break at the terminus.

The sergeant-major came up to me and said: "Are
you the man from staff headquarters?" and I said:
"Yes." He nodded; he looked pale and very young,
somewhat at a loss; I looked past him toward the dark,
scarcely distinguishable mass; all I could make out was
the gleaming trumpets of the band. "You wouldn't
happen to be a telephone operator?" asked the
sergeant-major, "we're short one here." "As a matter of fact I am," I said quickly and with an enthusiasm which seemed to surprise him, for he looked at me
doubtfully. "Yes, I'm one," I said, "I've had practical
training as a telephone operator." "Good," he said,
"you're just the man I need, slip in somewhere there at
the end, we'll arrange everything en route." I went over
toward the right where the dark gray was getting a
little lighter; as I got closer I even recognized some

faces. I took my place at the end of the company. Someone shouted: "Right turn—forward march!" and I had
hardly lifted my foot when they started playing their
"Must I then."

when the war was over

It was just getting light when we reached the German border: to our left, a broad river, to our right a forest, even from its edges you could tell how deep it was; silence fell in the boxcar; the train passed slowly over patched-up rails, past shelled houses, splintered telegraph poles. The little guy sitting next to me took off his glasses and polished them carefully.

"Christ," he whispered to me, "d'you have the slightest idea where we are?"

"Yes," I said, "the river you've just seen is known here as the Rhine, the forest you see over there on the right is called the Reich Forest—and we'll soon be getting into Cleves."

"D'you come from around here?"

"No, I don't." He was a nuisance; all night long he had driven me crazy with his high-pitched schoolboy's voice, he had told me how he had secretly read Brecht,

Tucholsky and Walter Benjamin, as well as Proust and
Karl Kraus; that he wanted to study sociology, and
theology too, and help create a new order for Germany,
and when we stopped at Nimwegen at daybreak and
someone said we were just coming to the German
border, he nervously asked us all if there was anyone
who would trade some thread for two cigarette butts,
and when no one said anything I offered to rip off my
collar tabs known—I believe—as insignia and turn
them into dark-green thread; I took off my tunic and
watched him carefully pick the things off with a bit of
metal, unravel them, and then actually start using the
thread to sew on his ensign's piping around his shoulder
straps. I asked him whether I might attribute this sewing job to the influence of Brecht, Tucholsky, Benjamin or Karl Kraus, or was it perhaps the subcon-
scious influence of Jünger which made him restore his
rank with Tom Thumb's weapon; he had flushed and
said he was through with Jünger, he had written him
off; now, as we approached Cleves, he stopped sewing
and sat down on the floor beside me, still holding Tom
Thumb's weapon.

"Cleves doesn't convey anything to me," he said,
"not a thing. How about you?"

"Oh yes," I said, "Lohengrin, 'Swan' margarine,
and Anne of Cleves, one of Henry the Eighth's wives."

"That's right," he said, "Lohengrin—although at

home we always had 'Sanella.' Don't you want the butts?"

"No," I said, "take them home for your father. I hope he'll punch you in the nose when you arrive with that piping on your shoulder."

"You don't understand," he said, "Prussia, Kleist, Frankfurt-on-the-Oder, Potsdam, Prince of Homburg, Berlin."

"Well," I said, "I believe it was quite a while ago that Prussia took Cleves—and somewhere over there on the other side of the Rhine there is a little town called Wesel."

"Oh of course," he said, "that's right, Schill."

"The Prussians never really established themselves beyond the Rhine," I said, "they only had two bridge-heads: Bonn and Koblenz."

"Prussia," he said.

"Blomberg," I said. "Need any more thread?" He flushed and was silent.

The train slowed down, everyone crowded round the open sliding door and looked at Cleves; English guards on the platform, casual and tough, bored yet alert: we were still prisoners; in the street a sign: To Cologne. Lohengrin's castle up there among the autumn trees. October on the Lower Rhine, Dutch sky; my cousins in Xanten, aunts in Kevelaer; the broad dialect and the smugglers' whispering in the taverns; St. Martin's Day processions, gingerbread men, Breughelesque carnival, and everywhere the smell, even where there was none, of honey cakes.

"I wish you'd try and understand," said the little guy beside me.

"Leave me alone," I said; although he wasn't a man yet, no doubt he soon would be, and that was why I hated him; he was offended and sat back on his heels to add the final stitches to his braid; I didn't even feel sorry for him: clumsily, his thumb smeared with blood, he pushed the needle through the blue cloth of his air force tunic; his glasses were so misted over I couldn't make out whether he was crying or whether it just looked like it; I was close to tears myself: in two hours, three at most, we would be in Cologne, and from there it was not far to the one I had married, the one whose voice had never sounded like marriage.

The woman emerged suddenly from behind the freight shed, and before the guards knew what was happening she was standing by our boxcar and unwrapping a blue cloth from what I first took to be a baby: a loaf of bread; she handed it to me, and I took it; it was heavy, I swayed for a moment and almost fell forward out of the train as it started moving; the bread was dark, still warm, and I wanted to call out "Thank you, thank you," but the words seemed ridiculous, and the train was moving faster now, so I stayed there on my knees with the heavy loaf in my arms; to this day all I know about the woman is that she was wearing a dark headscarf and was no longer young.

When I got up, clasping the loaf, it was quieter than ever in the boxcar; they were all looking at the bread, and under their stares it got heavier and heavier; I knew those eyes, I knew the mouths belonged to those eyes, and for months I had been wondering where the borderline runs between hatred and contempt, and I hadn't found the borderline; for a while I had divided them up into sewers-on and non-sewers-on, when we had been transferred from an American camp (where the wearing of rank insignia was prohibited) to an English one (where the wearing of rank insignia was permitted), and I had felt a certain fellow-feeling with the non-sewers-on till I found out they didn't even have any ranks whose insignia they could have sewn on; one of them, Egelhecht, had even tried to drum up a kind of court of honor that was to deny me the quality of being German (and I had wished that this court, which never convened, had actually had the power to deny me this quality). What they didn't know was that I hated them, Nazis and non-Nazis, not because of their sewing and their political views but because they were men, men of the same species as those

I had had to spend the last six years with; the words man and stupid had become almost identical for me.

In the background Egelhecht's voice said: "The first German bread—and he of all people is the one to get it."

He sounded as if he was almost sobbing, I wasn't far off it myself either, but they would never understand that it wasn't just because of the bread, or because by now we had crossed the German border, it was mainly because, for the first time in eight months, I had for one moment felt a woman's hand on my arm.

"No doubt," said Egelhecht in a low voice, "you will even deny the bread the quality of being German."

"Yes indeed," I said, "I shall employ a typical intellectual's trick and ask myself whether the flour this bread is made of doesn't perhaps come from Holland, England or America. Here you are," I said, "divide it up if you like."

Most of them I hated, many I didn't care about one way or the other, and Tom Thumb, who was now the last to join the ranks of the sewers-on, was beginning to be a nuisance, yet I felt it was the right thing to do, to share this loaf with them, I was sure it hadn't been meant only for me.

Egelhecht made his way slowly toward me: he was tall and thin, like me, and he was twenty-six, like me; for three months he had tried to make me see that a

nationalist wasn't a Nazi, that the words honor, loyalty, fatherland, decency, could never lose their value
—and I had always countered his impressive array of
words with just five: Wilhelm II, Papen, Hindenburg,
Blomberg, Keitel, and it had infuriated him that I
never mentioned Hitler, not even that first of May
when the sentry ran through the camp blaring through
a megaphone: "Hitler's dead, Hitler's dead!"

"Go ahead," I said, "divide up the bread."

"Number off," said Egelhecht. I handed him the
loaf, he took off his coat, laid it on the floor of the boxcar with the lining uppermost, smoothed the lining,
placed the bread on it, while the others numbered off
around us. "Thirty-two," said Tom Thumb, then
there was a silence. "Thirty-two," said Egelhecht,
looking at me, for it was up to me to say thirty-three;
but I didn't say it, I turned away and looked out: the
highway with the old trees: Napoleon's poplars, Napoleon's elms, like the ones I had rested under with my
brother when we rode from Weeze to the Dutch border
on our bikes to buy chocolate and cigarettes cheap.

I could sense that those behind me were terribly
offended; I saw the yellow road signs: To Kalkar, to
Xanten, to Geldern, heard behind me the sounds of
Egelhecht's tin knife, felt the offendedness swelling like
a thick cloud; they were always being offended for some
reason or other, they were offended if an English guard

offered them a cigarette, and they were offended if he did not; they were offended when I cursed Hitler, and Egelhecht was mortally offended when I did not curse Hitler; Tom Thumb had secretly read Benjamin and Brecht, Proust, Tucholsky and Karl Kraus, and when we crossed the German border he was sewing on his ensign's piping. I took the cigarette out of my pocket I had got in exchange for my staff Pfc chevron, turned around, and sat down beside Tom Thumb. I watched Egelhecht dividing up the loaf: first he cut it in half, then the halves in quarters, then each quarter again in eight parts. This way there would be a nice fat chunk for each man, a dark cube of bread which I figured would weigh about sixty grams.

Egelhecht was just quartering the last eighth, and each man, every one of them, knew that the ones who got the center pieces would get at least ten to five grams extra, because the loaf bulged in the middle and Egelhecht had cut the slices all the same thickness. But then he cut off the bulge of the two center slices and said: "Thirty-three—the youngest starts." Tom Thumb glanced at me, blushed, bent down, took a piece of bread and put it directly into his mouth; everything went smoothly till Bouvier, who had almost driven me crazy with his planes he was always talking about, had taken his piece of bread; now it should have been my turn, followed by Egelhecht, but I didn't move. I would

have liked to light my cigarette, but I had no matches
and nobody offered me one. Those who already had
their bread were scared and stopped chewing; the ones
who hadn't got their bread yet had no idea what was
happening, but they understood: I didn't want to share
the loaf with them; they were offended, while the others
(who already had their bread) were merely embarrassed; I tried to look outside: at Napoleon's poplars,
Napoleon's elms, at the tree-lined road with its gaps,
with Dutch sky caught in the gaps, but my attempt to
look unconcerned was not successful; I was scared of
the fight which was bound to start now; I wasn't much
good in a fight, and even if I had been it wouldn't have
helped, they would have beaten me up the way they did
in the camp near Brussels when I had said I would
rather be a dead Jew than a live German. I took the
cigarette out of my mouth, partly because it felt ridiculous, partly because I wanted to get it through the fight
intact, and I looked at Tom Thumb who, his face scarlet, was squatting on his heels beside me. Then Gugeler,
whose turn it would have been after Egelhecht, took his
piece of bread, put it directly into his mouth, and the
others took theirs; there were three pieces left when the
man came toward me whom I scarcely knew; he had not
joined our tent till we were in the camp near Brussels;
he was already old, nearly fifty, short, with a dark,
scarred face, and whenever we began to quarrel he

wouldn't say a word, he used to leave the tent and run along beside the barbed-wire fence like someone to whom this kind of trotting up and down is familiar. I didn't even know his first name; he wore some sort of faded tropical uniform, and civilian shoes. He came from the far end of the boxcar straight toward me, stopped in front of me and said in a surprisingly gentle voice: "Take the bread"—and when I didn't he shook his head and said: "You fellows have one hell of a talent for turning everything into a symbolic event. It's just bread, that's all, and the woman gave it to you, the woman—here you are." He picked up a piece of bread, pressed it into my right hand, which was hanging down helplessly, and squeezed my hand around it. His eyes were quite dark, not black, and his face wore the look of many prisons. I nodded, got my hand muscles moving so as to hold onto the bread; a deep sigh went through the car, Egelhecht took his bread, then the old man in the tropical uniform. "Damn it all," said the old fellow, "I've been away from Germany for twelve years, you're a crazy bunch, but I'm just beginning to understand you." Before I could put the bread into my mouth the train stopped, and we got out.

Open country, turnip fields, no trees; a few Belgian guards with the lion of Flanders on their caps and collars ran along beside the train calling: "All out, everybody out!"

Tom Thumb remained beside me; he polished his glasses, looked at the station sign, and said: "Weeze— does this also convey something to you?"

"Yes," I said, "it lies north of Kevelaer and west of Xanten."

"Oh yes," he said, "Kevelaer, Heinrich Heine."

"And Xanten: Siegfried, in case you've forgotten."

Aunt Helen, I thought. Weeze. Why hadn't we gone straight through to Cologne? There wasn't much left of Weeze other than a spattering of red bricks showing through the treetops. Aunt Helen had owned a fair- sized shop in Weeze, a regular village store, and every morning she used to slip some money into our pockets so we could go boating on the River Niers or ride over to Kevelaer on our bikes; the sermons on Sunday in church, roundly berating the smugglers and adulterers.

"Let's go," said the Belgian guard, "get a move on, or don't you want to get home?"

I went into the camp. First we had to file past an English officer who gave us a twenty-mark bill, for which we had to sign a receipt. Next we had to go to the doctor; he was a German, young, and grinned at us; he waited till twelve or fifteen of us were in the room, then said: "Anyone who is so sick that he can't go home today need only raise his hand." A few of us laughed at this terribly witty remark; then we filed past his table one by one, had our release papers stamped, and went out by the other door. I waited for a few moments by the open door and heard him say: "Anyone who is so sick that—," then moved on, heard the laughter when I was already at the far end of the corridor, and went to the next check point: this was an English corporal, standing out in the open next to an uncovered latrine. The corporal said: "Show me your paybooks and any papers you still have." He said this in German, and when they pulled out their paybooks he pointed to the latrine and told them to throw the books into it, adding, "Down the hatch!" and then most of them laughed at this witticism. It had struck me anyway that Germans suddenly seemed to have a sense of humor, so long as it was foreign humor: in camp even Egelhecht had laughed at the American captain who had pointed to the barbed-wire entanglement and said: "Don't take it so hard, boys, now you're free at last."

The English corporal asked me too about my papers, but all I had was my release; I had sold my paybook to an American for two cigarettes; so I said: "No papers" —and that made him as angry as the American corporal had been when I had answered his question: "Hitler Youth, S.A., or Party?" with: "No." He had yelled at me and put me on K.P., he had sworn at me and accused my grandmother of various sexual offences the nature of which, due to my insufficient knowledge of the American language, I was unable to ascertain; it made them furious when something didn't fit into their stereotyped categories. The English corporal went purple with rage, stood up and began to frisk me, and he didn't have to search long before he had found my diary: it was thick, cut from paperbags, stapled together, and in it I had written down everything that had happened to me from the middle of April till the end of September: from being taken prisoner by the American sergeant Stevenson to the final entry I had made in the train as we went through dismal Antwerp and I read on walls: *Vive le Roi!* There were more than a hundred paperbag pages, closely written, and the furious corporal took it from me, threw it into the latrine, and said: "Didn't I ask you for your papers?" Then I was allowed to go.

We stood crowded around the camp gate waiting for the Belgian trucks which were supposed to take us to Bonn. Bonn? Why Bonn, of all places? Someone said Cologne was closed off because it was contaminated by corpses, and someone else said we would have to clear away rubble for thirty or forty years, rubble, ruins, "and they aren't even going to give us trucks, we'll have to carry away the rubble in baskets." Luckily there was no one near me who I had shared a tent or sat in the boxcar with. The drivel coming from mouths I did not know was a shade less disgusting than if it had come from mouths I knew. Someone ahead of me said: "But then he didn't mind taking the loaf of bread from

the Jew," and another voice said: "Yes, they're the
kind of people who are going to set the tone." Someone
nudged me from behind and asked: "A hundred grams
of bread for a cigarette, how about it, eh?" and from
behind he thrust his hand in front of my face, and I saw
it was one of the pieces of bread Egelhecht had divided
up in the train. I shook my head. Someone else said:
"The Belgians are selling cigarettes at ten marks
apiece." To me that seemed very cheap: in camp the
Germans had sold cigarettes for a hundred and twenty
marks apiece. "Cigarettes anyone?" "Yes," I said, and
put my twenty-mark bill into an anonymous hand.

Everyone was trading with everyone else. It was the
only thing that seriously interested them. For two thousand marks and a threadbare uniform someone got a
civilian suit, the deal was concluded and clothes were
changed somewhere in the waiting crowd, and suddenly
I heard someone call out: "But of *course* the underpants go with the suit—and the tie too." Someone sold
his wristwatch for three thousand marks. The chief ar-
ticle of trade was soap. Those who had been in American camps had a lot of soap, twenty cakes some of them,
for they had been given soap every week but never any
water to wash in, and the ones who had been in the
English camps had no soap at all. The green and pink
cakes of soap went back and forth. Some of the men had
discovered their artistic aspirations and shaped the

soap into little dogs, cats, and gnomes, and now it
turned out that the artistic aspirations had lowered the
exchange value: unsculptured soap rated higher than
sculptured, a loss of weight being suspected in the
latter.

The anonymous hand into which I had placed the
twenty-mark bill actually reappeared and pressed two
cigarettes into my left hand, and I was almost touched
by so much honesty (but I was only almost touched till
I found out that the Belgians were selling cigarettes for
five marks; a hundred-per-cent profit was evidently regarded as a fair mark-up, especially among "comrades"). We stood there for about two hours, jammed
together, and all I remember is hands: trading hands,
passing soap from right to left, from left to right,
money from left to right and again from right to left;
it was as if I had fallen into a snakepit; hands from all
sides moved every which way, passing goods and money
over my shoulders and over my head in every direction.

Tom Thumb had managed to get close to me again.
He sat beside me on the floor of the Belgian truck driv-
ing to Kevelaer, through Kevelaer, to Krefeld, around
Krefeld to Neuss; there was silence over the fields, in
the towns, we saw hardly a soul and only a few animals,
and the dark autumn sky hung low; on my left sat Tom
Thumb, on my right the Belgian guard, and we looked

out over the tailboard at the road I knew so well: my
brother and I had often ridden our bicycles along it.
Tom Thumb kept trying to justify himself, but I cut
him off every time, and he kept trying to be clever;
there was no stopping him. "But Neuss," he said, "that
can't remind you of anything. What on earth could
Neuss remind anybody of?"

"Novesia Chocolate," I said, "sauerkraut and Qui-
rinus, but I don't suppose you ever heard of the The-
baic Legion."

"No, I haven't," he said, and blushed again.

I asked the Belgian guard if it was true that Cologne
was closed off, contaminated by corpses, and he said:
"No—but it's a mess all right, is that where you're
from?"

"Yes," I said.

"Be prepared for the worst . . . do you have any soap
left?"

"Yes, I have," I said.

"Here," he said, pulling a pack of tobacco out of his
pocket, he opened it and held out the pale yellow, fresh
fine-cut tobacco for me to smell. "It's yours for two
cakes of soap—fair enough?"

I nodded, felt around in my coat pocket for the soap,
gave him two cakes and put the tobacco in my pocket.
He gave me his submachine gun to hold while he hid the
soap in his pockets; he sighed as I handed it back to

him. "These lousy things," he said, "we'll have to go on carrying them around for a while yet. You fellows aren't half as badly off as you think. What are you crying about?"

I pointed toward the right: the Rhine. We were approaching Dormagen. I saw that Tom Thumb was about to open his mouth and said quickly: "For God's sake shut up, can't you? Shut up." He had probably wanted to ask me whether the Rhine reminded me of anything. Thank God he was deeply offended now and said no more till we got to Bonn.

In Cologne there were actually some houses still standing; somewhere I even saw a moving streetcar, some people too, women even: one of them waved to us; from the Neuss-Strasse we turned into the Ring avenues and drove along them, and I was waiting all the time for the tears, but they didn't come; even the insurance buildings on the avenue were in ruins, and all I could see of the Hohenstaufen Baths was a few pale-blue tiles. I was hoping all the time the truck would turn off somewhere to the right, for we had lived on the Carolingian Ring; but the truck did not turn, it drove down the Rings: Barbarossa Square, Saxon Ring, Salian Ring, and I tried not to look, and I wouldn't have looked if the truck convoy had not got into a traffic jam up front at Clovis Square and we hadn't stopped in front of the house we used to live in, so I did look. The term "totally destroyed" is misleading; only in rare cases is it possible to destroy a house totally: it has to be hit three or four times and, to make certain, it should then burn down; the house we used to live in was actually, according to official terminology, totally destroyed, but not in the technical sense. That is to say, I could still recognize it; the front door and the doorbells, and I submit that a house where it is still possible to recognize the front door and the doorbells has not, in the strict technical sense, been totally destroyed; but of the house we used to live in there was more to be recognized than the doorbells and the front door: two rooms in the basement were almost intact, on the mezzanine, absurdly enough, even three: a fragment of wall was supporting the third room which would probably not have passed a spirit-level test; our apartment on the second floor had only one room intact, but it was gaping open in front, toward the street; above this, a high, narrow gable reared up, bare, with empty window sockets; however, the interesting thing was that two men were moving around in our living-room as if their feet were on familiar ground; one of the men took a picture down from the wall, the Terborch print my father had been so fond of, walked to the front, carrying the picture, and showed it to a third man who was standing down below in front of the house, but this third man shook his head like someone who is not interested in an object being auctioned, and the man up above walked back with the Terborch and hung it up again on the wall; he even straightened the picture; I was touched by this mark of neatness—he even stepped back to make sure the picture was really hanging straight, then nodded in a satisfied way. Meanwhile the second man took the other picture off the wall: an engraving of Lochner's painting of the Cathedral, but this one also did not appear to please the third man standing down below; finally the first man, the one who had hung the Terborch back on the wall, came to the front, formed a megaphone with his hands and shouted: "Piano in sight!" and the man below laughed, nodded, likewise formed a megaphone with hands and shouted: "I'll get the straps." I could not see the piano, but I knew where it stood: on the right in the corner I couldn't see into and where the man with the Lochner picture was just disappearing.

"Whereabouts in Cologne did you live?" asked the Belgian guard.

"Oh, somewhere over there," I said, gesturing vaguely in the direction of the western suburbs.

"Thank God, now we're moving again," said the guard. He picked up his submachine gun, which he had placed on the floor of the truck, and straightened his cap. The lion of Flanders on the front of his cap was

rather dirty. As we turned into Clovis Square I could
see why there had been a traffic jam: some kind of raid
seemed to be going on. English military police cars were
all over the place, and civilians were standing in them
with their hands up, surrounded by a sizable crowd,
quiet yet tense: a surprisingly large number of people
in such a silent, ruined city.

"That's the black market," said the Belgian guard.
"Once in a while they come and clean it up."

Before we were even out of Cologne, while we were
still on the Bonn-Strasse, I fell asleep and I dreamed of
my mother's coffee mill: the coffee mill was being let
down on a strap by the man who had offered the Terborch without success, but the man below rejected the
coffee mill; the other man drew it up again, opened
the hall door and tried to screw the coffee mill onto
where it had hung before: immediately to the left of the
kitchen door, but now there was no wall there for him to
screw it onto, and still the man kept on trying (this
mark of tidiness touched me even in my dream). He
searched with the forefinger of his right hand for the
pegs, couldn't find them and raised his fist threaten-
ingly to the gray autumn sky which offered no support
for the coffee mill; finally he gave up, tied the strap
around the mill again, went to the front, let down the
coffee mill and offered it to the third man, who again

rejected it, and the other man pulled it up again, untied the strap and hid the coffee mill under his jacket as if it were a valuable object; then he began to wind up the strap, rolled it into a coil and threw it down into the third man's face. All this time I was worried about what could have happened to the man who had offered the Lochner without success, but I couldn't see him anywhere; something was preventing me from looking into the corner where the piano was, my father's desk, and I was upset at the thought that he might be reading my father's diaries. Now the man with the coffee mill was standing by the living room door trying to screw the coffee mill onto the door panel, he seemed absolutely determined to give the coffee mill a permanent resting place, and I was beginning to like him, even before I discovered he was one of our many friends whom my mother had comforted while they sat on the chair beneath the coffee mill, one of those who had been killed right at the beginning of the war in an air raid.

Before we got to Bonn the Belgian guard woke me up. "Come on," he said, "rub your eyes, freedom is at hand," and I straightened up and thought of all the people who had sat on the chair beneath my mother's coffee mill: truant schoolboys, whom she helped to overcome their fear of exams, Nazis whom she tried to enlighten, non-Nazis whom she tried to fortify: they had all sat on the chair beneath the coffee mill, had received comfort and censure, defense and respite, bitter words had destroyed their ideals and gentle words had offered them those things which would outlive the times: mercy to the weak, comfort to the persecuted.

The old cemetery, the market square, the university. Bonn. Through the Koblenz Gate and into the park. "So long," said the Belgian guard, and Tom Thumb with his tired child's face said: "Drop me a line some time." "All right," I said, "I'll send you my complete Tucholsky."

"Wonderful," he said, "and your Kleist too?"

"No," I said, "only the ones I have duplicates of."

On the other side of the barricade, through which we were finally released, a man was standing between two big laundry baskets; in one he had a lot of apples, in the other a few cakes of soap; he shouted: "Vitamins, my friends, one apple—one cake of soap!" And I could feel my mouth watering; I had quite forgotten what apples looked like; I gave him a cake of soap, was handed an apple, and bit into it at once; I stood there watching the others come out; there was no need for him to call out now: it was a wordless exchange; he would take an apple out of the basket, be handed a cake of soap, and throw the soap into the empty basket; there was a dull thud when the soap landed; not everyone took an apple, not everyone had any soap, but the transaction was as swift as in a self-service store, and by the time I had just finished my apple he already had his soap basket half full. The whole thing took place swiftly and smoothly and without a word, and even the ones who were very economical and very calculating couldn't resist the sight of the apples, and I began to feel sorry for them. Home was welcoming its home-comers so warmly with vitamins.

It took me a long time to find a phone in Bonn; finally a girl in the post office told me that the only people to get phones were doctors and priests, and even then only those who hadn't been Nazis. "They're scared stiff of the Nazi Werewolf underground," she said. "I s'pose you wouldn't have a cigarette for me?" I took my pack of tobacco out of my pocket and said: "Shall I roll one for you?", but she said no, she could do it herself, and I watched her take a cigarette paper out of her coat pocket and quickly and deftly roll herself a firm cigarette. "Who do you want to call?" she said, and I said: "My wife," and she laughed and said I didn't look married at all. I also rolled myself a cigarette and asked her whether there was any chance of selling some soap; I needed money, train fare, and didn't have a pfennig. "Soap," she said, "let's have a look." I felt around in my coat lining and pulled out some soap, and she snatched it out of my hand, sniffed it, and said: "Real

Palmolive! That's worth—worth—I'll give you fifty marks for it." I looked at her in amazement, and she said: "Yes, I know, you can get as much as eighty for it, but I can't afford that." I didn't want to take the fifty marks, but she insisted, she thrust the note into my coat pocket and ran out of the post office; she was quite pretty, with that hungry prettiness which lends a girl's voice a certain sharpness.

What struck me most of all, in the post office and as I walked slowly on through Bonn, was the fact that nowhere was there a student wearing colored ribbons, and the smells: everyone smelled terrible, all the rooms smelled terrible, and I could see why the girl was so crazy about the soap; I went to the station, tried to find out how I could get to Oberkerschenbach (that was where the one I married lived), but nobody could tell me; all I knew was that it was a little place somewhere in the Eifel district not too far from Bonn; there weren't any maps anywhere either, where I could have looked it up; no doubt they had been banned on account of the Nazi Werewolves. I always like to know where a place is, and it bothered me that I knew nothing definite about this place Oberkerschenbach and couldn't find out anything definite. In my mind I went over all the Bonn addresses I knew but there wasn't a single doctor or a single priest among them; finally I remembered a professor of theology I had called on with a friend just

before the war; he had had some sort of trouble with
Rome and the Index, and we had gone to see him simply
to give him our moral support; I couldn't remember the
name of the street, but I knew where it was, and I
walked along the Poppelsdorf Avenue, turned left, then
left again, found the house and was relieved to read the
name on the door.

The professor came to the door himself; he had aged
a great deal, he was thin and bent, his hair quite white.
I said: "You won't remember me, Professor, I came to
see you some years ago when you had that stink with
Rome and the Index—can I speak to you for a moment?" He laughed when I said stink, and said: "Of
course," when I had finished, and I followed him into
his study; I noticed it no longer smelled of tobacco,
otherwise it was still just the same with all the books,
files, and house plants. I told the professor I had heard
that the only people who got phones were priests and
doctors, and I simply had to call my wife; he heard me
out—a very rare thing—then said that, although he
was a priest, he was not one of those who had a phone,
for: "You see," he said, "I am not a pastor." "Perhaps
you're a Werewolf," I said; I offered him some tobacco,
and I felt sorry for him when I saw how he looked at my
tobacco; I am always sorry for old people who have to
go without something they like. His hands trembled as
he filled his pipe, and they did not tremble just because

he was old. When he had at last got it lit—I had no
matches and couldn't help him—he told me that doctors
and priests were not the only people with phones.
"These night clubs they're opening up everywhere for
the soldiers," they had them, too, and I might try in
one of these night clubs; there was one just around the
corner. He wept when I put a few pipefuls of tobacco
on his desk as I left, and he asked me as his tears fell
whether I knew what I was doing, and I said, yes, I
knew, and I suggested he accept the few pipefuls of
tobacco as a belated tribute to the courage he had
shown toward Rome all those years ago. I would have
liked to give him some soap as well, I still had five or six
pieces in my coat lining, but I was afraid his heart
would burst with joy; he was so old and frail.

"Night club" was a nice way of putting it; but I
didn't mind that so much as the English sentry at the
door of this night club. He was very young and eyed me
severely as I stopped beside him. He pointed to the
notice prohibiting Germans from entering this night
club, but I told him my sister worked there, I had just
returned to my beloved fatherland and my sister had
the house key. He asked me what my sister's name was,
and it seemed safest to give the most German of all
German girls' names, and I said: "Gretchen"; oh yes,
he said, that was the blonde one, and let me go in;
instead of bothering to describe the interior, I refer the

reader to the pertinent "Fräulein literature" and to movies and TV; I won't even bother to describe Gretchen (see above); the main thing was that Gretchen was surprisingly quick in the uptake and, in exchange for a cake of Palmolive, was willing to make a phone call to the priest's house in Kerschenbach (which I hoped existed) and have the one I had married called to the phone. Gretchen spoke fluent English on the phone and told me her boy friend would try to do it through the army exchange, it would be quicker. While we were waiting I offered her some tobacco, but she had something better; I tried to pay her the agreed fee of a cake of soap in advance, but she said no, she didn't want it after all, she would rather not take anything, and when I insisted on paying she began to cry and confided that one of her brothers was a prisoner of war, the other one dead, and I felt sorry for her, for it is not pleasant when girls like Gretchen cry; she even let on that she was a Catholic, and just as she was about to get her first communion picture out of a drawer the phone rang, and Gretchen lifted the receiver and said: "Reverend," but I had already heard that it was not a man's voice. "Just a moment," Gretchen said and handed me the receiver. I was so excited I couldn't hold the receiver, in fact I dropped it, fortunately onto Gretchen's lap; she picked it up, held it against my ear, and I said: "Hallo—is that you?"

"Yes," she said, "—Darling, where are you?"

"I'm in Bonn," I said, "the war's over—for me."

"My God," she said, "I can't believe it. No—it's not true."

"It is true," I said, "it is—did you get my postcard?"

"No," she said, "what postcard?"

"When we were taken prisoner—we were allowed to write one postcard."

"No," she said, "for the last eight months I haven't had the slightest idea where you were."

"Those bastards," I said, "those dirty bastards—listen, just tell me where Kerschenbach is."

"I,"—she was crying so hard she couldn't speak, I heard her sobbing and gulping till at last she was able to whisper: "—at the station in Bonn, I'll meet you," then I could no longer hear her, someone said something in English that I didn't understand.

Gretchen put the receiver to her ear, listened a moment, shook her head and replaced it. I looked at her and knew I couldn't offer her the soap now. I couldn't even say "Thank you," the words seemed ridiculous. I lifted my arms helplessly and went out.

I walked back to the station, in my ear the woman's voice which had never sounded like marriage.

EUROPEAN CLASSICS

Honoré de Balzac	*The Bureaucrats*
Heinrich Böll	*Absent without Leave* *And Never Said a Word* *And Where Were You, Adam?* *The Bread of Those Early Years* *End of a Mission* *Irish Journal* *Missing Persons and Other Essays* *A Soldier's Legacy* *The Train Was on Time* *Women in a River Landscape*
Madeleine Bourdouxhe	*La Femme de Gilles*
Lydia Chukovskaya	*Sofia Petrovna*
Grazia Deledda	*After the Divorce* *Elias Portolu*
Aleksandr Druzhinin	*Polinka Saks • The Story of Aleksei Dmitrich*
Venedikt Erofeev	*Moscow to the End of the Line*
Konstantin Fedin	*Cities and Years*
Fyodor Vasilievich Gladkov	*Cement*
I. Grekova	*The Ship of Widows*
Marek Hlasko	*The Eighth Day of the Week*
Bohumil Hrabal	*Closely Watched Trains*
Erich Kästner	*Fabian: The Story of a Moralist*
Ignacy Krasicki	*The Adventures of Mr. Nicholas Wisdom*
Miroslav Krleža	*The Return of Philip Latinowicz*
Karin Michaëlis	*The Dangerous Age*
Andrey Platonov	*The Foundation Pit*
Arthur Schnitzler	*The Road to the Open*
Ludvík Vaculík	*The Axe*
Vladimir Voinovich	*The Life & Extraordinary Adventures of Private Ivan Chonkin* *Pretender to the Throne*